MANWHORE

A FERRO FAMILY SHORT STORY

BY:

H.M. WARD

WWW.HMWARD.COM

COPYRIGHT

H.M. WARD PRESS
First Edition: December 2015
ISBN: 9781630350987

MANWHORE

Chapter 1

This trial is becoming a nightmare. Even as I sit across the aisle from a man accused of doing horrendous things to his wife, I find myself questioning whether he really did them or not. Like the rest of the opposing counsel, I've seen the crime scene photos and, no matter what I do, I can't erase them from my mind. That beautiful man with his dark hair and blue eyes sits across from me day after day, expressionless, his hands folded serenely in his lap. He shows no contempt, no remorse.

Nothing.

I've combed through his past, spoken to his previous lovers—all women from before his marriage to the deceased—and they tell me this man is not the Sean Ferro they knew. The Sean Ferro they knew was kind and compassionate, full of life.

He laughed easily and gave his love freely. Their version of him does not mesh with the shell of a man that I've studied across the courtroom these past months.

Mr. Ferro is clean-shaven, his hair smoothed back into a perfect frame for his vacant blue eyes. There's something about him that's utterly intimidating, but the vibe I get when I'm around him is off. It's as if I can sense the two men living within that gorgeous hollow shell.

The counselor sitting next to me is convinced that weird vibe implies guilt. All of my coworkers are way past wondering if he's guilty. They believe, beyond the shadow of a doubt, that he is. I'm not so sure anymore.

During our preparations for the trial, I played the role of devil's advocate. Basically, my job was to anticipate the defending counsel's strategy for making the jury believe Sean Ferro is innocent. It turns out I was excellent in that role—so good, in fact, that I began to believe in the possibility of his innocence.

Is the man sitting across the aisle from me guilty of murdering his pregnant wife?

"Objection." David Cunning sits in the first chair to my left. He jumps to his feet, making a passionate plea while waving his hands in the air as if this is a matter of life and death. "She's leading the witness."

Before the judge can reply, the opposition says, "Withdrawn."

Susanna Titleman is a named partner at the most prestigious law firm in New York City. She's a tall, thin woman with jet-black hair. She wears it slicked back into a neat chignon that rests at the nape of her neck. The slim skirt of her charcoal gray suit forms perfect leading lines down her long, lean legs. Coupled with a pair of Armani pumps, she looks like she walked straight off the Harvard Law school billboard.

While in law school, we all thought we'd change the world—and that, like Susanna, we'd look awesome while doing it. We also thought we'd get paid enough to live off of, maybe even enough afford things like that suit. It's ok, though. I've since learned the good guy isn't supposed to be rich. Working for the District Attorney's office means I rent an apartment I can barely afford and own a closet full of bargain basement suits. My heels are designer irregulars from Nordstrom Rack. My makeup is Maybelline. Despite my frugality, it's still been hard to repay my loans and afford to live. Nobody said any of this in law school. We were so focused on saving the world that we missed the fine print—you can't be a good guy without taking a vow of poverty.

It's been hours since we stopped for lunch. The sun is setting behind the tall glass and steel buildings, causing their shadows to creep across the marble courtroom floor. In all this time, Mr. Ferro has not moved. Others have also noticed and speculated it's because he's incapable of grief. They think he sits here day in and day out, not feeling a thing.

But sitting second chair has given me a front-row seat, and I know that's not true. Whether he committed murder or not, the man can feel. If I hadn't been sitting here I wouldn't believe it either, but here I am, close enough to observe his ice blue eyes thaw when they exhibited pictures of his dead wife and child. His mouth didn't move. His jaw didn't tighten. He never loosened the grip of his hands, and he never stopped staring straight ahead. Sitting this close and studying those eyes, I could see the pain of loss and the desolation of grief. His refusal to move isn't callousness—it's a survival instinct. He's frozen himself in time, locked himself in that night, and he can't escape.

Since I noticed these things, I've watched him more carefully. As I've played devil's advocate during preparations, I've become increasingly intrigued by the man sitting across the courtroom from me. Sean Ferro has erected walls of steel around himself. He'll never let anyone in again. I know that, I can see it, and as I sit here, day in and day out, I'm unconvinced that I'm on the right side.

Everyone thinks he's guilty—and I mean everyone, from random people on the street, to

Amanda's parents, to his own mother. I thought he was guilty, too—until I started to notice things about him.

The gavel slams down and echoes through the courtroom, interrupting my thoughts. "That's all for today."

The judge is an older man with dark gray hair, a round face, and a big nose. He's highly educated, but when he speaks he sounds like a sanitation worker. A lot of people think this is intentional, as his political values lean toward defending the common man. His political values do not make him more lenient in his decisions, though, and he's earned a reputation for being a hard-ass.

A guy like Sean Ferro doesn't stand a chance in this courtroom, but attempts to obtain a change of venue, a change of judge, a change of anything were all denied. Being privileged may be enjoyable for Mr. Ferro on the outside, but in this courtroom the judge will fault him for it.

David looks over at me and smiles widely. He lifts his case notes from the desk and taps them down into a neat stack before slipping them into his attaché case.

"That went well. I don't know how you do it, Paige, but your insight has been priceless in this trial."

I smile and nod, accepting the praise with grace as I slip my notepad into my bag. It's a Vera Bradley, also an irregular. I couldn't figure out why until I put it on my shoulder and realized one strap is longer than the other. If I stand slightly lopsided the bag looks right, and it makes me look impatient and annoyed, so I blend right in with the other New York City residents.

"Sure, no problem."

I don't know how I do it either, and the whole thing is starting to take a toll on me. To see things from Sean Ferro's side means I need to get inside his head. It's not just a matter of arguing from the opposite side of the courtroom and pretending to be the defense. The rest of my associates think it's easy, that all I need to do is put my feet into the opposing attorney's shoes—but it's so much more than that.

Once I slip into Sean Ferro's mind, my argument is bulletproof, my plan of action is ironclad. I'm the one who suggested using his blank stare against him. I'm the one responsible for him being labeled a monster. When the press spoke to David about the shock seen on Mr. Ferro's face, it was me who suggested it was arrogance instead. The press took my subtle suggestions and ran wild. Suddenly my words are everywhere, flowing freely from the mouths of every news anchor in the city. Mr. Ferro was deemed a monster beyond comprehension, showing absolutely no remorse for his wife and child. Since Mr. Ferro refuses to speak on the matter, even to defend himself, the hype surrounding the trial grows bigger and bigger.

Even as he stands up, our day in court concluded, the defendant doesn't look around the courtroom. He acts as if the other people aren't here. A sympathetic person might believe this man is dying inside, but there are no sympathetic people here. Everyone around him now believes the story I created. They believe he is a cold and distant husband who killed his wife and unborn child on a whim. They see his contempt as indifference and think this man doesn't care about life at all. Even if Sean Ferro manages to escape jail, he's already been given a life sentence by society. This city will never forget what he did. He will live the rest of his life alone, disgraced, and feared.

David stands there watching me. He clears his throat, loosens his tie and asks, "How about drinks? You and me blowing off some steam? Maybe you can tell me what's going on inside that prim and proper little head of yours?"

My jaw drops open, and I make a strangled noise. The last thing I am is prim and proper, but they don't know that. I laugh it off and act like he's joking.

"You know the rules, no fraternizing is allowed. If you haven't noticed, I really need this job."

David smiles and runs a hand through his blonde hair. "Drinks with a colleague is okay, Paige. What we do beyond that is up to you."

David is a few years older than me, with a long, lean body, sandy blonde hair, and bright green eyes. He thinks everyone we prosecute is guilty beyond a shadow of a doubt, and he wants to nail their asses to the wall. Everything is black and white to him. There are no shades of gray, no room for the law to be unclear. I wish I had his certainty because everything seems gray to me.

I laugh and wag a finger in his face as I pass him. "Nice try, Romeo, but you're not my type."

David feigns hurt as he follows me down the aisle. "Even if not with me, you should take tonight off, blow off some steam. We've been working our asses off, and there's no way this deviant is going to walk. Seriously, give yourself a break."

"That sounds good."

"I mean it, no work." David disappears down the hallway weaving amongst people without another word.

Chapter 2

I find Jess draped over the arm of the sofa, blonde hair cascading to the floor where it pools. She's tapping her foot and singing along with music I can't hear. Kicking off my shoes, I pad across the worn carpet and plop down next to her head.

Jess screams and jolts upright, taking a swing at me as she moves.

"Get off!" Her fist connects with my hip as she rounds on me.

I shriek and jump back as another fist comes flying my way. I grab it before it can connect and jerk her arm forward, making her faceplant against the couch. Before she can regroup, I swing my leg up and straddle her back. She's laying facedown in the cushions and swearing up a storm. Breathless, I yell, "It's me, dumbass!"

She shrieks something I can't make out, but relaxes enough for me to know I'm safe from attack. I roll off of her, yank down my skirt and smooth my blouse. Jess sits up. Her hair covers her entire face making her resemble a golden version of Cousin It.

"You suck!" She huffs and bats at her long hair until it flips over her shoulders and falls down her back.

I laugh. Surprising Jess is easy and happens too frequently to count.

"Yeah, well, that's debatable." I pick at the run in my stocking and frown.

Jess takes a calming breath the same way she teaches her students in yoga class. People who know us both think *she's* the crazy one. If they knew what I do to blow off steam, they'd reconsider. But that's my secret—even from Jess.

Jess sits Kumbaya-style, placing her hands palms up on her knees. She breathes in, holds the breath in her lungs, and then dramatically releases it. After repeating the process several times, she looks over at me with a lethargic smile.

"So, how was your day?"

"Lovely. I single-handedly crucified a man's reputation, had the DA hit on me, and got punched in the hip by my yogi roommate who never hits anything except me."

"You snuck up on me!" She drops her hands and her back curves like a sulky teenager. "Fine, I was spaced out, but you know how Journey affects me! I get lost in the glorious haze of 80's music. I can't stop believing, Paige. I gotta hang on to this feeling!"

I snort-laugh and grab a pillow before sinking back into the couch. "You're a dork."

"You need to go out." Jess shoots a worried smile in my direction. "I can hear your aura screaming for attention. It's freaky. What'd you do today?" She scoots closer to me and starts swatting at my aura as if it were visible. I stare at her. She's like a human cat. I want to tape a laser pen to the topside of the ceiling fan and randomly turn it on just to see what she would do.

"Jess, you can't just swat away the invisible crap that's messing with my force field. I'm still going to be moody."

She stops, drops her hands to her lap, and shakes her head.

"Then you do it. Visit your happy place—though you might need to bring ID just in case they don't recognize you."

I grin. "Shut up. And it's not my happy place."

"Well, call it whatever you want, but when you come home, you are always way happier. Where do you go anyway?"

She tucks her bare feet under her pink yoga-panted butt as she watches me. I try to act like it's not a big deal. I shrug and grab a magazine off the coffee table. Opening it, I sit back and scan the pages. "Nowhere special. Even if I did have a so-called happy place, I'm too tired to go there right now."

"And grumpy. And mad. And maybe even," she reaches up over my head and snatches something invisible out of the air. She holds it in her hand as if it were real and grimaces. When she meets my gaze again, she adds, "remorseful? That can't be right. You enjoy making people miserable for a living. I'm the one who patches them up. We're yin and yang. I'm light and fluffy bunnies, while you're black holes and grunge."

"Grunge?" I laugh and point to my suit. "What about my outfit says grunge?"

"That's not what I mean. I'm talking about your spirit, your soul. That thing inside you that you abuse day in and day out. That thing is getting beaten beyond recognition. The case you're working on right now is about a wife killer. You should want to make him suffer, so what's with the pity?"

The last word is like an icy spike in my spine. I sit up and pull away from her, wishing I could run. I laugh nervously, knowing she sees through me.

"I don't pity him. He deserves everything coming to him and more."

She's quiet for a moment, and I feel her gaze on the side of my face. When she talks again, her voice is soft and careful.

"That may be true, but after everything you went

through with your mom I'd understand."

"You'd understand what?"

"How much you want to make sure guys like that don't hurt anyone else. How much it stings when some of the guilty ones still walk away. How much it hurts to remember your mom, and—"

I cut her off, unable to hear it right now. I stand and snap at her, "Don't go there."

But she doesn't stop. "—and how she died. Her death rules your life, Paige. She wouldn't want that."

"You didn't know her." My voice is quiet and gruff, nearly a growl. My eyes narrow to thin slits, and it's taking everything in me not to lash out at her. Jess is my friend, but she has no idea what it feels like to see her mother crying on the floor, covered in blood, gasping for air but unable to breathe. I can still hear Mom begging, and that agonizing gurgling sound fills my head, even now. I helplessly watched her die, and there wasn't a damned thing I could do to stop it.

Jess stands slowly and lifts her hands, palms toward me.

"I don't want to fight. I just know how invested you are in this case. I can see you're worn thin, and I don't want this to destroy you. I love you, Paige."

Now I feel like an asshole. My lips twist into a scowl because she's right. I hate it when she's right.

"Fine, I get it, okay. You need to realize there's more to it than that. Life isn't so simple, and things aren't that black and white."

"I know, and I get it." She nods and offers a careful smile. "I just don't want to see you suffering like this."

"This topic isn't open for discussion. Drop it."

"Paige."

"I said stop!"

"You can't keep pretending that your past has no bearing on your future. It does!" She's pleading with me now, and I can't bear it.

Without a word, I head for the door. I grab my shoes with one hand and my purse in the other.

"Stop running! You need to talk with someone, Paige. If not with me, then someone else. Anyone!" She follows me to the door and calls after me, but I don't look back.

There's a cab parked at the curb, waiting for a fare. I jump in and give the address. He nods and pulls into traffic. My stomach sinks into my shoes. I'm not ready for this.

Not tonight.

Chapter 3

Maybe I'll just sit at the bar.

Maybe I won't go back there.

I push through the door with my heart beating hard. Every time I walk through those doors is just as intimidating as the first time. On the outside, I'm confident—hard, even. On the inside, I'm falling apart. Maybe I should do it. I need to stop thinking for a while, stop feeling the fear that strangles me.

Jess's words bounce around in my head like drunk Ping-Pong balls. Their movements make no logical progression. I just see them hopping from my mother's memory to Sean Ferro, and it disturbs me. I don't know why I'm comparing them, but for some reason I see a connection. I wish I knew why.

As I step over the threshold, the familiar scent fills my lungs and makes forgotten sensations come rushing back. I hate this place, but I love it. I need it. When things get like this, when I can't find my way around my own mind anymore, I find myself here. My dealings with the district attorney's office make this risky, though. That's part of the reason I haven't come in so long.

There was a time when this place was the only way to get my mother out of my mind. I was sixteen when she died. I was eighteen when a friend first took me here. At twenty-three I'm still not over it. The people I met here in the beginning have moved on, found other vices. For me, this isn't a fetish—it's not something to do or not do—it just is.

I walk toward the black glass bar, past the tables with white linens and romantic music. This place embodies the nine levels of love, from pretty to perverted. The further back, the deeper you explore the building, the more likely you are to meet someone who's into what you're into. The bar in the front divides the happy-go-lucky types from the darker crowd. I know I belong in the back, but right now I just want a drink.

I pull up a stool and gesture to the bartender. There's a decent number of people here, and almost every spot at the bar is taken. When I get my order, I tip my head back and shoot it in one smooth gulp. I slap the glass down on the bar and order another. I intend on sipping this one, and pick up the freshly filled shot glass. When I press it to my lips, I sense someone watching me. I glance around and see him.

My heart stops.

I can't breathe.

I don't move.

Bright blue eyes lock with mine and pin me in place. Sean Ferro sits at a small, expensive private table across from me. He's alone, still wearing his suit from earlier. The tie is tight, and his jacket is still on. He has a bottle of amber liquid in an ice bucket and a crystal glass in his hand. His lips form a straight line, and his jaw is locked.

Fuck. I slam down the second drink and turn back to the bar. Maybe he'll leave. I'm not leaving. I've never seen him here before. I would have thought a reporter or someone would have used this to smear him by now.

Before I can order a third drink, I'm given one.

"Compliments of that gentleman." The bartender points over my head to the table where Mr. Ferro still sits.

I nod once and follow the protocol. A drink means interest. My accepting it means I'll comply. I know the rules here. I grab my purse with one hand, the glass with the other, and walk over to his table.

Being here is stupid. If anyone sees me, I'm screwed. I'll lose my job, and everyone will know I'm completely messed up.

I wipe all emotion from my face and slip into the booth across from him. I set the drink on the table and stare at the beautiful man. Those sapphire eyes swim with heartache, but they're hardening. It's getting harder to see it.

When he speaks, his voice is deeper than I remember. "Are you following me, Miss Driskill?"

I'm not, but if I say I'm not, he'll know I'm here for the same reason he is. So, I lie.

"Yes, of course. It's my job to know about everything you do."

"So you can use it against me in court?" He says it like we're discussing the weather. He's emotionally distanced himself from the conversation, from me.

"That's the plan." I lift my cup and grin. "Thanks for this."

He nods and watches me as I press the glass to my lips. The liquid burns as it slides down my throat. When I finish, I place the shot glass on the table and prepare to stand with every intention of walking away.

But Ferro's piercing eyes are trained directly on mine and, when he speaks, I can't remember what I was doing. "You're not following me. If you were, I'd never have seen you. Give me a little more credit, Miss Driskill. Additionally, there's no way you plan on reporting my presence in a place like this. You'd have to explain why you were here, and why you've already had more to drink than is socially acceptable. So tell me, why are you at Club Noir this evening?"

I stand stunned into silence. The longer he speaks, the more I want to hear. What the hell is wrong with me? I shake it off and let a lazy smile fill my face.

Leaning forward, I look at him from under my lashes. "The truth, Mr. Ferro, is simple and presumably the same reason you're here."

He doesn't move. He doesn't lean in, mirror my smile, or speak. He's perfectly still, watching me, waiting for the explanation I won't give.

I expect him to deny it, but he doesn't. I breathe in slowly, watching the muscles in his jaw tighten. His hands are in front of me, holding the glass. He's not white-knuckled, so he's controlling that temper very well. He does have a temper. I've seen pictures of him, hands in the air, screaming, his chiseled face twisted with rage. He hides his thoughts well, now, much better than when the trial began.

I tap my pointer finger on the table once, then twice. On the third tap, he reaches out and covers my hand with his, stopping the movement.

"I know why you're here."

The breath is sucked from my lungs. Those azure eyes bore into me, and I feel trapped. His hand grows hotter and heavier as it rests on top of mine. I want to run, but I don't. I sit there, waiting for him to say words I can't hear—words I'll never say myself. I swallow hard and watch him, waiting for the rest of his thoughts to come spilling over those sexy lips.

I hate him. Why'd he have to be right here, right now? Damn it!

I fake a smirk. "Really? Then tell me. Why am I here?"

Sean glances to the side and then tips his head forward. The corner of his mouth twitches as if he wants to smile. He presses my hand harder to the table, and I let him.

"Level Nine. You're here for the activities on nine."

Chapter 4

My heart slams into my ribs and falls to my feet. I start to pull my hand away, but he holds onto me.

"I should go." My voice sounds hesitant.

"You should stay, and show me around." His voice is softer than before, more careful. He lifts his palm from my hand and returns it to his drink. That suit fits him well, accentuating his lean body. I wonder what he looks like under all those clothes, what his skin would feel like beneath my hands.

No.

I shake my head and push the thought away.

"No, I don't think so. I don't work with beginners."

"Who said I'm a beginner?" Sean leans forward, and I feel his foot slide between mine. My knees separate slightly. His touch feels charged. I wish I could feel more, but I shouldn't.

There's something about him I can't quite put my finger on, and it has nothing to do with the murder. Prior to Amanda, Sean Ferro was a manwhore. He had a different co-ed on his arm every night. He slept with everyone and loved no one. Then—poof!—he was a committed husband for years. The District Attorney's dossier on Sean Ferro includes tons of dirt—just none from during his marriage to Amanda. Either the man is a mastermind...

Or he truly loved her.

I want to know which one. Curiosity is going to kill me, assuming David doesn't when he finds out I was here.

My gaze sweeps over Sean once again, considering. Would it be so bad? What if I could find out if he really did it? That would abate my guilt regarding the public perception I've fostered toward him.

"Miss Driskill, you can stay, or you can go—it's all the same to me. You know what happens here just as well as I do, though I don't frequent this place as often as you."

"I don't frequent Club Noir." I spit out the words, irritated, enunciating each one as disgust clouds my face. "Screw off, Ferro." The alcohol is dulling my senses, but still I know I need to leave. I can't be here, not with him. Not now, not ever.

He's so calm, so completely in control of

himself. He leans back in the booth, placing one arm on the backrest and surveying me with those gorgeous eyes.

"Go, then. No one is holding you here." The corners of his lips twitch into a smirk. "As much as you'd enjoy it."

I roll my eyes and decide to leave. At the same moment, a woman stops in front of the table and blocks me in. She leans toward Sean, acting like I'm invisible. She pulls the collar of her shirt down—way down—revealing ample cleavage beneath a pink collar set with two gleaming gemstones. If she falls into that set of DDD falsies, she'll drown.

"I'm looking for a partner tonight. Come on back." Her massive Louis Vuitton bag swings forward, slapping me in the head as she pulls away.

"Hey!" I snap, pushing the purse out of my face. "Watch what you're doing."

Her overinflated lips snake into a smile. "Oh, I am. Better try again, honey. This one is mine."

Sean says nothing. He sits there watching, his eyes moving slowly between the two of us. If he thinks I'm going to fight some bimbo for him, he's out of his mind. At the same time, I'm not letting her think she's better than me. I reach into my purse and pull out my own collar. It's black leather and studded with nine gems.

"This thing is so bulky," I say, placing the collar on the table with a thud, then digging deeper into my bag. I pull a packet of mints from the bottom and pop one into my mouth.

Her jaw drops, and she looks at me again, I mean really looks.

"So, the librarian type does get all the action?"

"More than the Barbie type. Everyone knows what they're getting when it's all hanging out." I point at the twins, which seem ready to burst out of her blouse.

Sean's gaze drops to the table and lands on my collar. He reaches for it and lifts it reverently. "This is the highest level here, is it not?"

The woman nods.

"And the gems, there aren't more she can receive—are there?" He brushes his thumb over the center stone. It's a black diamond. I wonder if he knows how I earned that one. Most women don't have that—Barbie included. She sucks in a breathy gasp and puts on her pouty lips.

"I might not have as many, but that just makes me more eager to please. I'll be in the back, waiting for you." She says the last sentence in a porn star voice. She probably is a porn star. "Bye, sugar. Good luck."

My gaze narrows and I'm seriously considering slamming my fist into her nose job. Sean's voice pulls me from my thoughts.

"Keep your hands to yourself, Miss Driskill. You won't like the consequences. Club Noir isn't the type of establishment that enjoys a chick fight."

"Good night, Mr. Ferro," I say with a laugh as I stand up from the table. "Have a lovely time fucking a real Barbie doll—because that never gets old." I roll my eyes and toss down a twenty. "For my drink."

"I wouldn't know. I don't have an affinity for plastics. They seem crass, but maybe that's just me."

My face contorts. I want to hit him. Sure, people have accused me of being gay, but I'm not. I may have tried it once, but that was a long time ago. Based on how he said it, I think he knows that, though. I freeze my face and lock my emotions away.

I fold my arms across my chest and blurt out, "What do you want?"

"You have memories you'd prefer to forget. So do I."

I cock one hip to the side and shoot death rays at his heart with my eyes. "Find a different partner. I'm not your type. You couldn't survive me."

He swallows hard, an unintended movement. He's still holding my collar, and I can't leave without it. I did all sorts of things to earn that, and I won't toss it away like trash. I unfold my arms and tap the table once, pressing my finger against the dark wood indicating I want the collar—now.

He looks down at the center gem and rubs it with his thumb, slowly in small circles. The sensations he evokes overload my senses, and I can't stand here anymore. I reach across the table and snatch it away from him. "That's as close as you'll ever get to touching me."

"Of course, Miss Driskill. Have a good evening." He lifts his glass and sips his drink.

As I rush to leave, I hear another woman trying to entice him. Before I push through the door, I look back into the room. If he went with her, I'd be able to see his back following her down the long hallway.

The corridor is dressed in gold and black. Amber lights dim softly against the walls making it look like a passage into Heaven.

It's empty.

Chapter 5

A week passes at zombie speed. In my attempt to release my frustration, I destroy my favorite dildo. It's no wonder why I don't have a boyfriend. Guys probably sense I could break their junk and avoid me to keep their jewels safe. I should reconsider being a lesbian. There are no body parts on a woman to snap off accidentally. Too bad I like men.

My attention is barked back to the present by the tone in the DA's voice. David is nearly yelling, "But the problem is that he sounds distressed. You can clearly hear him swallow a sob. The jury is going to eat that up! The bastard planned it. We need to prove his tone during the call was all an act."

Janna Bent is an older woman with frizzy dirty blonde hair that curls uncontrollably. She's a little thick around the middle, but has a killer rack and a pretty face. She's also a bitch on steroids when it comes to winning.

"So we don't use it!" She's sitting across from David, on the other side of his desk in a well-used chair.

"Then they will! This recording is already admitted into evidence. We've been over this, Janna." David slams his hands down on his desk. He inhales sharply and looks up at me. I've been quietly sitting in the corner, picking at the hem of my skirt. "What would you do, Paige?"

He likes that I'm definitive and that I usually have an answer ready to go, but this time I don't. I buy time. I drop the fabric and look up at him. "Play me the recording again, please."

He presses the button, and I listen. Through the cheap speaker, Sean Ferro makes a strangled noise, as if his voice won't come out. With the sound of his voice, an image forms in my head. I picture him crying silently, cradling his dead wife in his arms, and not noticing her blood stain his hands and clothes. And if I can see it, the jury will, too.

Without that part at the beginning, the remainder of the call sounds stoic, precise, like a man thinking clearly. I push up and walk across the room to David's desk. I stop the recording and play the beginning a second time. I play it and stop. Play it and stop. I'm sitting on the edge of his desk, staring into space, and consider it.

"What are you thinking, Paige?" David knows by the expression on my face that I've thought of something. The problem is that I'm not sure if I can be this horrible of a person. What if Sean really was cradling her body? What if he really was crying?

This angle will destroy him completely. Any empathy he has left will be eradicated. My eyes sweep the room, considering the stacks of papers and hours of research spent building a case to nail this man. In all that time, we couldn't find anything to prove, beyond the shadow of a doubt, that he planned his wife's murder or that he committed it. Nothing except his being the one to find her in the crime scene. The pieces of this puzzle fit both ways.

I blink a few times and stop the recording. I can't listen to his voice like that anymore. Sean Ferro doesn't sound like that. There's no control in the tone of the recording. It's like he's trying to hold back tears—or another equally jarring emotion.

I say it. I say it because I have to crush him. I have to come at him with everything and know I did my job to the best of my ability.

"He's laughing."

"What? No, he isn't." Janna sits up and grabs the recording. She presses the button, and her eyes light up. A smile spreads across her face. "Oh, my God! He is. He's trying not to laugh. That sick son of a bitch." Her jaw hangs open, and words fail her.

David takes the recorder and replays the call

again and again. He's staring at the metal box in his hands without seeing it. He's picturing the jury and their reaction to my suggestion.

"We need a story to go with this, to make it real for the jury. Comb back through the case files and find out what Sean Ferro was doing the night of the murder."

I nod, slip off the desk, and pick up the police report. Before I open it, I turn back and tell them the rest of my plan. "Get him to laugh, just once, while he's on the stand. Then play the recording. The jury will hear it, and you won't need a story—they'll believe for themselves."

Chapter 6

The pit of my stomach is sinking. I feel like I'm going to be sick, and that's not something that happens to me often. When I was a girl, my mother joked that my stomach must be made of steel. I could eat anything, then go on a carnival ride, get whipped every which way, and jump off, only to stuff my face more.

But this isn't a carnival ride. Maybe that's the problem.

I'm destroying someone's life and it's not because I'm certain he did it. How did I get to this point? Why am I willing to flush away my principles for a crappy paycheck? Nailing a Ferro for murder would bring more notoriety, more opportunities. But can I live with myself, condemning a possibly innocent man?

I finish painting my face and grab my leather jacket before heading out. Jess is coming up the stairs as I'm rushing down them. I'm in the right frame of mind, and I can't let her soften me.

"Hey, Jess. I'm headed out to work for a little bit, but I saved you some fried chicken. I ate all the biscuits."

She grabs my arm, stopping me. "Look at you! Hot thang!" She grins as she visibly checks me out. Then she teases, "You mean you saved me chicken because you ate bread for dinner again? Are you turning Vegan or something?"

I laugh. Loudly. "No! I just—"

She finishes my sentence, "—love buttermilk biscuits and can't control yourself. Got it. Thanks for the chicken! See you later! You look hot tonight, Paige!"

As I race down the stairs, I call back to her, "Thanks!"

The air is crisp, and it smells like snow. I tuck my chin into my coat and run down the street to a cab. I slip into the back seat and tell the cabby, "54th and Madison Avenue." He nods and takes off. The traffic isn't too bad, so the ride won't be long. The cabbie does his thing, and I get lost in my thoughts.

I haven't done this in months. Approaching Ferro is suicide, isn't it?

My gut is saying no, but my head is screaming yes.

There's something about the guy that puts my nerves on edge. If I've learned anything, it's that primal reactions shouldn't be ignored. There's something there, something dark and dangerous beneath his plastic smile and perfect manners. I intend on finding out what it is, where he really was the night his wife was killed—because I don't think he told the cops the whole story and the gun is still missing.

Occam's Razor is usually right, the simplest explanation is often the truth, but I can't swallow this explanation. It's almost as if Ferro wants us to believe he killed her. He never refutes the charges. He's never offended. Add in visiting a club a few times per week during the trial—specifically, an establishment known for connecting people with singular tastes—and damn! He's either incredibly stupid or completely genius.

The cab pulls up to the curb and stops. The driver looks up in the rearview mirror. "Club Noir."

I hand him the fare and slide out of the cab, smoothing my small tight skirt, and adjusting my jacket as I go. The wind whips my hair into my eyes, so I look down until I reach for the door. At the same time I tug it open, someone is coming through. The glass door opens forcefully, causing me to stagger backward. The heel of my thigh high boot catches a crack in the pavement, and my balance is lost. I'm flailing, frantically trying to right myself, when a warm hand firmly grips my arm. I'm pulled forward, and crash into a firm, muscular chest wrapped in a luxuriously soft black coat.

My fingers splay across the fine wool coat buttoned midway up, a cobalt blue scarf tucked into the opening at the top. I glance up and gasp, suddenly realizing it's him—Sean Ferro.

His voice is sinfully deep, rumbling beneath my fingertips as he speaks.

"Apologies. I didn't see you there."

I mean to step back and shake him off, but he doesn't move. His hands remain fixed above my elbows, and his indigo eyes darken as if he's thinking about my skin against his skin, slick and hot. I make sure my voice comes out clearly, even though I'm insanely nervous.

"I didn't see you either. Sorry about that."

He's still holding me, a breath away. If I leaned in, I could taste his lips. They're smooth and full, and perfectly pink. I wonder how he kisses, if it's soft or hard, playful or intense. My gaze lingers on his mouth, and I shiver involuntarily. His thumb rubs against my arm in a slow circle.

"If you're ok…" His voice trails off like he wants to say more, but he doesn't.

I'm suddenly very aware of how fast I'm breathing. It sounds way too loud in my ears, but I can't help noticing his chest rise as he gasps for air. What the hell is happening? This was going to be a controlled pairing. I was supposed to come to the club and whip out my collar. I wasn't supposed to slobber all over him on the sidewalk.

I nod, unable to find words, and wonder where all my gusto goes when it gets sucked away. From the looks of it, this encounter has shaken him as well. His gaze fixes on my lips, and he's visibly fighting the pull between us. I want to press my body to his and feel him writhing beneath me. I want things I shouldn't want. This attraction wasn't part of my plan. As long as he's touching me, I can't think.

I twist my shoulders slightly, causing him to release his hold on my arms. He collects himself and looks over his shoulder at the black Bentley sitting at the curb. There's a light dusting of stubble on his jaw and, for once, it isn't clenched tight. He presses his lips together, then looks back at me.

The wind blows his dark hair into his eyes. Extending his hand, he commands, "Come with me."

Chapter 7

I follow him into the backseat of the car and slide across the bench. He slips in behind me and slams the door. My heart races harder, faster, as my breathing becomes too ragged. It's hard to feign confidence when Sean can see what he does to me.

When I glance up at him, wondering what he wants to say, I force my spine straight and relax the muscles in my face. Sean hasn't glanced away from me since he slammed into me coming out of Club Noir. The way his brows rest slightly lifted on his beautiful face makes me want to reach out and touch him. But I don't. I remain still with my hands folded neatly in my lap.

I glance past Sean and see the driver standing outside the car as if waiting for something. Before I know what's happening, Sean's warm hand is on my chin, redirecting my face so that my gaze meets his. My chest fills with too many emotions at once. The attraction is intense and being this close is like holding two magnets together, but not allowing them to touch. The pull becomes more pronounced, and all those feelings continue to rise. I want to lean into his hand and press my lips to his.

While my control flies away into the night, Sean's remains completely intact. He tips my face one way and then the other as if he were examining livestock.

I jerk away and frown. "I'm not a horse."

"No one said you were."

"What do you want, Mr. Ferro? I have places to be and this—as lovely as it is—wasn't among my plans for the evening." My tone is curt, irritated. It's the only way I can hide the firestorm of emotions burning through me.

"Really? Weren't you coming to take part in Club Noir? Find a partner? Fuck your troubles away?"

I reach for the door, intending on leaving without responding. Sean moves quickly, taking me by my shoulders and twisting me back toward him. He doesn't wait for me to say anything. Before I know what's happening, he's in my space, within a breath of me. He stays there, watching my lips, letting the pull between us build.

My insides twist and, I can't help it, a small gasp escapes from between my lips. It's as if that was what he wanted, because he closes the distance between us and presses his mouth to mine. His lips are soft and perfect as he lingers in a chaste kiss, barely touching me. The result is intense. Desire shoots through my body like a bolt of lightning, making me want to do everything all at once.

I'm losing control. That's worrisome and exciting. It's like standing on the top of a lightning rod and waving a metal rake around during a storm. It's not a matter of if I'll get struck—it's inevitable.

When Sean is involved, every ounce of control I possess vanishes. I see it now, and it scares me. Something is very wrong with this situation, and it's not just that I'm part of the team trying to throw his ass in jail—we're enemies. He should hate me, but this kiss says something else entirely. A jolt of reality pours down my spine like ice.

Breathless, I wriggle away and stare at him with an intensity I normally hide. Two worlds are colliding in my mind. Reality and Club Noir. Normally, they exist separately. They don't converge. Hell, they don't even touch. I find it difficult to believe that this meeting is an accident, that Sean Ferro is only searching for solace at Club Noir.

I wipe my mouth with the back of my hand, still mere inches away from him. "You know as well as I do this isn't possible."

Sean's expression is placid, all smoothness, as if

the kiss left him unbothered, unaffected. "Go on. Say what's on your mind." Those eyes reveal too much. As I look into them, I fall deeper and deeper. I sense his excitement and the worry that barely pinches his brow. I can taste the disappointment building in the back of his mouth. I can feel the way his walls become thicker by the second, as if building an impenetrable keep inside a fortress to conceal his heart forever.

But right now, there are cracks in the façade revealing his thoughts, allowing all this emotion to flow out like shafts of light piercing the darkness.

My jaw hangs open, frozen. The moment is too intense, and panic is clawing at my insides, wanting to rise and take over. I shove it down and swallow hard. "If my boss finds out I was in your car, I'll be fired. But this—if he saw this—if he knew you were here, and I was here…"

Sean looks me over and calmly explains, "Mr. Cunning—that's a laughable name by the way—doesn't appear to be the sort to frequent Club Noir, and, if he were, he'd already have known about your darker pursuits. What would possibly make him venture here, now?"

My heart is slapping against my ribs, making it hard to breathe. My palms are sweaty, and the remnants of my composure wash away. "I don't know! Why are you here now? Why is anyone here now?"

He doesn't answer.

I wring my hands in my lap and glance out the window. My panic is real now, not imagined. I need Club Noir, but not when it means Sean Ferro comes with it.

Lips trembling, I mutter, "I lost my thoughtful spot."

Sean nearly chokes as he tries to swallow a laugh. "I'm sorry, you're thoughtful—"

I wave my index finger in his face and cut him off. "Stop coming here!"

"I could ask the same of you." Those calm blue eyes are hypnotic. They're like the ocean, vibrant, ever-changing, and with depths beyond comprehension. "But I won't."

My eyes cut to Sean and then back to the Club. I make a strangled sound in the back of my throat. "I knew exactly what I was going to do tonight until you hit me with the door."

"Then do it, find someone who shares your preferences." His eyes bore into me as the silence builds between us. He's still so close, his scent filling my head, making me crazy.

"Don't follow me." I reach for the car door again, and this time Sean doesn't stop me.

I push the door shut and walk around to the curb, hellbent on finding a partner in Club Noir.

Chapter 8

Every inch of my skin hums, demanding to be touched, while my mind blurs with memories I'd rather forget.

I march through the glass doors, past the black bar, and down the golden hallway. I pass the women and men proceeding with caution and lacking my determination. Is that what this is? It's almost like I have to prove to myself that I can still do this. Where did that come from?

I make it to the elevator bank and pull out my collar for the guard. He's an older guy with a big nose and gruff voice. "Put it on if you want to go up. You know the rules." He's wearing a black suit with a name tag that says GABE.

I lift my hair and tighten the collar around my neck. "I know."

He pushes the button and calls the elevator. As he stands there, a timid couple walks up behind me. The woman has a white collar on with no stones. The man is giddy and a bit younger than her. She smiles at me nervously. I wonder which of them wanted to come here.

When the elevator arrives and the door chimes, I walk through. Gabe swipes a key card allowing me to select any floor. When the couple tries to enter, Gabe stops them. "Sorry, novices aren't allowed upstairs without an upper-level."

The woman smiles nervously and watches me. My finger is hovering over a button, but I've not pressed it yet. She sees my black collar, as does the guy she's with. I act on a whim, reaching out for her hand and pulling her forward. "She's with me."

Gabe nods and steps back. "She's your responsibility for the evening."

"I know." I press the button, and before her man can follow us into the elevator, Gabe blocks him.

"Sorry, but you know the rules. You need a guarantor."

"But, we're together." The man points at the woman in the white collar, very excited and very annoyed that he's going to miss out.

Gabe shakes his head and scolds the man as the elevator doors close. I quickly press every button for every floor and then lean back against the railing. "I'm going to nine, but you don't have to. You should probably observe on two and see if this is your thing."

Her eyes nearly bug out of her head. "You're going to nine?"

I nod. "Yes, and you should get off here." The doors open and the pale blue lights spill into the room. She doesn't move. The doors slide shut, and we continue up another floor.

I shake my head, allowing my hair to fall into my eyes. "You shouldn't be here."

"Why did you say that?" She laughs nervously and tucks a strand of red hair behind her pale ear.

"It's not your thing. You're afraid."

"So. Aren't you?" She's visibly trembling by this point.

I feel bad for her. "No, I'm not. I'm here because I want to be. I think you're here because that guy wanted it. This isn't for everyone. What's your name, anyway?"

"Claire." She looks at the floor and seems sad. "We've been together for a long time, and I don't want to lose him. If I have to start doing this, well, how do I do it?"

I groan inwardly. That is the worst possible reason to show up here. "As a voyeur. Then try some of the mini public shows. If that doesn't make you leave, try the third floor. But not before watching."

"Can I watch you?" Her face turns bright red when she asks me. I want to smash my head into the wall for pulling her up here with me. "Please?"

I glance over at her again and consider it. She won't be in the way and maybe if she sees what I'm into she'll think twice about doing something like this for someone else. "Fine, but don't ask me anything until later."

Claire smiles and nods. "I can do that. So, where are we going?"

"Apparently to the fourth-floor lounge. I need to find a partner and sign you in."

I feel skittish tonight. That meeting with Ferro has my head spinning. I can't concentrate on the newbie—or anything else for that matter. The doors slide open, and I head over to the desk in the golden room and check in.

Behind the counter is a tall, extremely thin man with a shaved head. His lanky body is covered in tattoos and piercings. "It'll be about an hour before we can get you on stage. There aren't too many niners here tonight. What kind of partner do you want?"

Claire whispers to me, "What's a niner?"

The man laughs and shakes his head. "How'd you get stuck with her?"

"A niner is a black collar, someone who's done all this before," I tell her before responding to the guy. "Don't be a prick. Everyone starts somewhere."

"And you're Mother Teresa helping her out like this. Club Noir thanks you for making a new patron."

His tone is somewhere between sarcastic and serious. "So, for you, oh, I see a good one—unless you already have a partner in mind?"

"Just assign someone."

He types quickly into the computer and then says, "Done." We're both given a keycard and allowed to roam the floor in public and private areas.

I walk straight back with the newbie on my heels, slowing as we approach a seating area around a stage. Two women are up there right now. One has a cane in her hand. She's wearing a dark leather bodysuit. The other woman is laying on the couch, face down, watching the audience, wearing only a leather harness. Her pale cheeks flush red, and several raised welts mark her thighs. They're almost done.

I sit at a small table toward the back, one reserved for black collars and their tops. Claire tries to sit next to me. "No, over there. You have to stand and watch."

She nods and backs away, standing by the wall. She winces when the cane comes down. Her eyes widen, shocked, as the sound of it striking flesh makes other viewers lean in. I remember doing this. I liked being on the receiving end, but not the cane—I preferred the cat. The way the tails feel stinging nine different places at once makes it impossible to think about anything else.

That's what this place is for—to forget. The

people who have lived the darkest lives turn up here, ready to banish their pain, hoping it never returns. But it comes back, which is why I have every level, every stone. The pain never stops because life never lets it.

As I watch the last delicious strike of the rod, I notice tears streaming silently down the bottom's cheeks. She may enjoy the idea of being a bottom—a submissive—but Club Noir isn't her thing. It stuns me how many people wander in here, how many people will go this far for someone else when they can't bear it.

I'm a different story. I want something to feel, something that makes sense to me. I understand this. It's action and reaction. It also forces the bottom— the person in the slave role—to learn how to conceal their emotions. The master is called the 'top' here. The patrons flip roles between 'tops and bottoms,' doing whichever they please, and it sounds a little less scary than, 'dominant and submissive.' The actions are far from cute, though. Being a bottom isn't for everyone, but it helped me hide the horrors that were so evident on my face all those years ago.

I order a cocktail and lean back in my chair. After it's gone, I shuck my leather coat, revealing my collar, leather bralette and mini skirt, and shiny black thigh high boots. It's warm in here.

The music pulses and the golden lights flash. The stage curtain drops.

Claire rushes up behind me, whispering, "When it's your turn, are you taking me with you? I don't think I can do that." She's visibly shuddering and turning a shade of green. I feel sorry for her.

"You should go home," I say firmly.

"I can't."

"I won't do anything with you or to you. I only signed me up. You just stand by the wall all night. When you can't stand anymore, leave." I speak sternly, not looking her in the eye until the end.

Claire nods and resumes her position at the wall behind me. We watch another couple and then a trio. The hour passes quickly. I head to the back room to get ready and meet my partner. We need to go over any rules or safe words ahead of time. Most people have a firm line they won't cross. If we don't talk about it before time, there's no way to know when to stop.

As I head to the backstage area, I see a couple doing more than they should. I look away, rushing past them. Sex in public spaces is a no-no. Sex, in general, is a no-no here. The owner will kill them when she finds out. And she will find out.

I walk into the women's changing room. It's decorated with soft silvers and shades of gray with lots of mirrors and warm light. There are white locking cubbies to store my things. One wall has costumes hanging on a long silver rod running the entire length of the wall. There are sheer dresses, revealing lingerie, harnesses, and more. Anything you could possibly want to put on the perfect show. And the price tags that dangle from each indicate they cost more than my weekly check.

I can take anything I want—Level Nine perk—but decide to remain in the clothes I'm wearing. I sit down in front of a mirror and braid my hair so that it's not falling in my face. As I do so, I hear the other women in the room talking.

A brunette with ample cleavage dusts blush across her cheek and then says, "I didn't see him either, but Angie said he's here." Her accent is thick, like the water in Jersey.

There's another woman next to her, spraying enough hairspray to form a lingering cloud. Her accent is dually thick. "Lots of guys are here, but not too many leave the main floor."

"I'm not new! He's in the waiting room. Can you imagine? Sean Ferro on stage!" She's giddy.

I drop my hairbrush and jump up quickly.

He is not.

He did not.

I'm going to…

Chapter 9

I want to scream. I rush out of the changing room and race down the hallway to the waiting area. Sean's standing there, shirtless, with dark slacks and a belt around his narrow waist. In the golden light, the muscles of his back are defined perfectly under smooth pale skin.

I walk up behind Sean and shove him hard. "What the hell?"

Sean turns around and looks at me. "No touching, Miss Driskill. We're following my rules tonight."

"The hell we are!"

Sean watches me, his face devoid of emotion as he calmly steps closer. I step back. "You know how this goes. Unless you want to lose face in front of your peers, you'll do as I tell you."

"You asked for me? What'd you do, follow me

inside?" I go to shove him again, but he grabs my wrists. When I try to jerk away, he leans in close, tugging me until we are nose-to-nose.

"I left. When I returned, I signed in downstairs—where I remained until a few moments ago. They didn't tell me which bottom I was with, so stop acting like you matter. You don't." He tosses my hands back and steps away.

I stand there, stunned, jaw hanging open for half a beat before I snap it shut again. "I'm not doing this with you."

"Then pay the penalty and move on." There's no trace of anger in his voice. It's simply gone.

Sean pads away from me, and I notice he's barefoot. I don't want him like this, not here. I need to make him leave. I pull out the only thing I can think of. "They will crucify you in court. You can't do this and walk away. You can't go onto the stage, subdue a woman, and whip her! You shouldn't be doing any public anything right now. What's wrong with you? You're a smart man—you should understand this is suicide!" I'm practically yelling, and my hands are waving around like a crazy person.

He arches a dark eyebrow at me. "Why do you care?"

"I don't."

"Then let's go over the rules and get out there. What's your safe word?"

I stare at him, shocked. I'm too surprised to

think, so the word tumbles out. "Aardvark."

Sean looks down at me and laughs. "Seriously?"

"You won't hear it again, so don't bother teasing me about it. Listen, if you want to walk away, I won't report it. Actually, I can cover it up. Everyone saw me walk in with a newbie. I'll show her a few things, and she can take your spot. I'll say it was a computer glitch."

Sean steps toward me. I slide away again. He takes another step, and I back away once more. We do it a few more times until my back hits the wall. Sean presses against me, close enough to whisper in my ear, "I don't need your help."

"Why are you doing this?"

"I'm already dead, remember? I'm a monster. It's time I show the world who I really am and stop denying it."

My stomach twists as he throws those words in my face. It's as if he knows I'm the one who started those rumors. I grab his wrist and yank him in the other direction, but he won't move. I growl. "Fine. If you want to be a dumbass and do it in front of as many people as possible, follow me into the web room."

He hesitates. "The room with the live feed?"

I tug again. "That's the one. I have a very pretty mask, and they have very elaborate dungeon sets. You can pick your torture chamber and set it free on the Internet."

Sean nods as if determined and follows me down the hall. All of the doors are unmarked, or this wouldn't work. I have no idea what I'm going to do once I get him inside, but I can't let him do this. I have to try something.

When we come to the door, I swipe my keycard. It's the only thing that will open the lock from either side. I hold the door open and am grateful there's only one dim glowing red light inside. "There's no going back."

Sean turns and looks at me, equally stubborn and committed. I hold the door open and gesture for him to walk inside. As he passes me, I hold my keycard behind my back, fold it in half, and press hard. It snaps. I drop it to the floor and step inside, allowing the door to lock behind me.

Chapter 10

Sean pads to the center of the room and turns slowly, the red light spilling over his pale skin like blood. He stands beneath the bare bulb, shirtless. His chest rises with each breath and makes me notice his taut nipples.

As our eyes adjust to the dim light, it becomes increasingly evident we are not in the web room. Though now used for storage, this room was once a Level Nine playroom. The walls and ceilings still boast their original racks, but now hang full of out of date and infrequently used items. The old grates now have handcuffs, satin ribbons, rope, and other bindings hanging down from the grid.

His jaw tightens, and he steps toward me. "You did this on purpose."

I stand my ground. "Yes. You're behaving

erratically."

He says nothing. His eyes bore into me, filling me with ice. I can't see the depths this time. I can't read him at all. Pulse hammering in my ears, I explain. "There are better ways to control your emotions. Saying fuck it and making sure the world sees you're the monster they think you are will backfire."

"How?" His strong arms fold over his firm chest. He's listening. And angry.

"Because they'll get hung up on the sexual acts. They'll think less of you, not be more frightened. You crave power and control. But if you make your actions at Club Noir public, no one will fear you. They'll think you're a deviant, and that's all."

He's closer now, inching toward me. He towers above me, and I know this was stupid. It's probably some sort of misplaced guilt about labeling him as a monster in the first place. He wouldn't be setting himself on fire and showing the world if I hadn't made the world think it first.

He watches me from beneath thick, dark lashes. "No, they won't."

I insist. "Yes, they will. But, if you keep it a secret, if no one knows, you can control everything. You can have moments of peace, retain power, and keep the world wondering how much they should fear you. That's the better plan."

"How often do you come here?" The shift in his

tone is noticeable. He's no longer playing defense. Something changed.

My mouth hangs open. "I, uh, not much. Not recently."

He nods and steps away. Sean slips his hands into his pockets and hangs his head. He paces as he speaks. "I haven't done anything like this in a long time. I've had images in my mind, things that I feel in my arms, in my hands, that I need to do. It's not a want, Miss Driskill, it's a need. I feel like I'm suffocating and you're the only one who sees it." He turns on his heel and glances up at me.

My stomach dips as my heart pounds harder. My skin prickles all over as if something bad were about to happen. Sean steps toward me one pace at a time, and says, "Tell me what to do." He stops in front of me and waits.

Shaking my head, I laugh nervously and step away. Hands up, palms toward him, I back away another step. "I don't know what you mean."

"I think you do." He steps closer.

"I don't."

I step away until my back hits the empty metal rack bolted to the wall. The steel bars feel like ice on my bare skin. I swallow hard as Sean takes one hand and then the next and holds them on either side of my head, pressing lightly. "Teach me how to forget what I've seen. I know you can do it. I know you figured out how to wash the memories away. That's all I want, a moment without seeing her body covered in blood. A moment without—" he swallows hard, sucking in air and forcing his chest to press against mine. "Without hearing her beg me to come home. I want to forget what happened to us that night, what I lost. Because I lost everything and no matter what the trial outcome is, it's my fault. This nightmare never ends. My mind never stops thinking of things I could have done differently. If I'd called, if I'd taken her away, if I'd—"

I can't stand it anymore. The pain within him pierces his voice, ripping him apart in front of me. Every moment he breathes, he's in agony. I understand because I live the same lie. I look serene on the outside, but there's only turmoil within.

I pull my wrist out of his grip and press my finger to his lips. "I get it. I wish I didn't, but I do."

In that moment, I feel it. This mutual understanding is the footing of friendship. It could turn into something, but I know it can't. Not with him. He's trying so hard to forget who he is and what he's endured that there will be nothing left of him if he goes through with this.

"Then teach me what you do. I've seen you in court. I've seen you smiling and acting like nothing weighs you down. I know that's not true, so how do you find solace?"

It's like he punched me in the stomach. The part of me that I try so hard to hide is completely visible to him. "I'm not sure I can teach you what you want to know. I'm a ghost of who I was before. Part of it is letting yourself wither. If you have no soul, it doesn't hurt as much."

He nods and then steps back. "I died with Amanda. I'm not looking for healing—I just want to survive living."

It's becoming more evident that I'm going to be with him. That's what he's asking me, to show him how to find a sexual escape. If I do this, if anyone finds out about my being with Ferro, I'll never work again. At the same time, I remember being where he is, so close to the event and still feeling so raw. I wanted that period of my life to vanish, and it took so long to figure out how to make that happen.

Sean steps toward me and falls to his knees. He lowers his head, making it clear he's submitting to me. "Please, Paige…help me."

The words, the way he pleads so softly, decides it for me. I breathe his name as he kneels at my feet. I've never felt so powerful before in my life. The great Sean Ferro is at my feet, begging me for help. It should fill me with pride and make me feel powerful, but it doesn't. The reason why is simple— no matter what I do, I can't heal his heart.

Chapter 11

We start with the simple things, after stripping him and going over the rules. He says he has no limits, no hard lines. I don't press him. As he stands there wearing absolutely nothing, it's difficult not to look at him. Normally, I wouldn't, but he's so beautiful. Every inch of his body is perfect. If I keep thinking about it I won't be able to do this. It's not about sex—it's about control.

I grab a pair of handcuffs and reach for Sean's wrist. His lips part and he breathes slowly. I feel his eyes on the side of my face as I reach up and cuff him to the overhead grate. As I work, my arm brushes against his cheek and I wish I could kiss him.

Ignore the naked part. Humiliation is part of being the bottom. He's naked, and I'm not. It's not sexual, at least it's not supposed to be, but I feel so pulled to him. I scold myself and try to snap out of it.

I don't blindfold him because I need to see his face. I go over a few basics that pertain to me and then add, "Do not speak unless I tell you to. Do you understand?"

His eyes are downcast, and he's careful not to look at me. "Yes."

We play a few games, and I'm quickly learning that nothing pulls his mind from his past. He remains far away, the vacant look still in his eyes. I tell him not to hide it from me. I keep trying different things, kicking the pain level up as I go. We're way past novice, and I'm getting nowhere.

I've lashed him, caned him, dripped hot wax down his back, but he doesn't react. It's as if he lost the ability to feel anything. Most tops would become harsher now, hitting harder, using clamps, and trying to reach a point where it's evident that the bottom feels something. My gut impression says that won't work with Sean.

I change tactics. I'm going to break the rules. He's chained in place and until now, I haven't touched him. I can't do so without it being sexual. I don't trust myself. But maybe that's the problem. We both sense this about each other. Maybe I should follow my instincts and see where we end up.

I walk around his body, dragging the pads of my fingers over his bare hips. He inhales sharply, but says nothing. I continue to skim my fingers over him, circling around to the smooth skin and toned muscle of his back. His narrow hips curve into a sexy ass that's tight and perfect. His legs are long and lean with enough muscle to pin a girl in place.

"Should I stop?"

Sean is tense, finally on edge. It's the tender touches that do it. He shakes his head and swallows hard. His voice is faint. "Go on."

I remain behind him, lingering for a moment. I follow my impulse and press my cheek to his back. I slide my hands down his sides as I listen to his heart beating fast within his chest. I lower my lashes and allow them to touch his skin. He gasps like he was hit by a truck.

What happened to make him like this? Tenderness is what sets him on edge. That can't be right. I need to do something different and test my theory further. There's one action that's so personal that I want to try it.

I hesitate in front of him and stare at the floor. I shouldn't do this. It's crossing a line. But…

His head is still lowered, hanging between his broad shoulders. "Do whatever you're thinking. It's the only way to find out."

This is wrong.

I shouldn't be here.

I can't be with him.

I can't do this.

But I am.

I bend my knees and slowly lower myself in front of his waist. I'm still wearing my outfit, minus the jacket, and kneeling in front of his perfect package. Leaning in close, I close my eyes and exhale slowly, letting my hot breath wash over him. He lets out a small moan, which makes me wonder.

There's an element missing, something I need, and I know he needs it, too. I feel it. I glance up at him and catch his eye. His hands are chained above his head, and he tries to look away quickly. It's supposed to be like that, but not this time.

I rise slowly, and gently press my body to his as I stand. I take his face in my hands and force him to look at me. "Sean, do you like edge play?"

"Level Nine so soon?" He sounds disappointed.

"Not quite. I'm deviating from the norm. So I guess, the question is this—do you trust me?"

Edge play is when you push your partner to their limit. One of the most common forms is asphyxiation. It requires a great deal of trust because the ramifications when performed incorrectly are disastrous.

I accidentally brush his skin with my finger. His eyes focus sharply, and it's as if my touch was painful. Sean's weakness isn't air; it's gentleness.

As the thought fills my mind I realize that I've found it—I discovered the Sean Ferro cocktail that will make him forget everything.

Chapter 12

Sean's eyes lock on mine. My heart beats so hard I think he must hear it. He's frozen in place, as if he knows I've found something. He doesn't speak, he only nods.

"What's your safe word? Because I won't stop."

He shakes his head. "Don't stop. If you think you found something, do it. You're the only woman in here with a Level Nine collar and that jewel. I trust you."

I press my lips together and swallow hard. I splay both hands on his chest and touch him lightly. I trace the curves of his chest, slowly sliding my fingers over the rise and fall of his body. I trace the lines leading to his pecs and following them down to his abs. I run a finger along each muscle, tracing it softly. My mouth waters as I think about kissing him there, along his stomach, and dragging my tongue along his skin.

It's a lover's caress and he hates it, well part of him can't stand it. The other part is completely erect and begging to be touched. Sean grits his teeth as I touch him, trying not to cry out. The muscles in his neck cord tightly as he fights the sensation.

I ask, "What are you feeling?"

"I can't—" He hisses through his teeth, unable to speak. I feel like I should stop, but I'm sure I've found it.

A bead of sweat rolls down his temple and drips onto the floor. There's a spreader bar between his ankles to hold his legs apart and then each ankle is chained to the floor. He is beautiful. I wonder what he was like before all this happened. If he enjoyed such light touches from his wife, or if he was a tender lover. I'll never know.

The only thing I'm certain of is that this will sharpen his senses. He'll hone in on how to own me, how to destroy me. The challenge is all consuming, and leaves no thought for anything else. I know because I'm doing it to him now. Seeing him fight me is erotic and thinking about taking him in my mouth is such a bad idea—it's against the club rules. It's against our agreement. It defies everything because I'm stealing his control. His panic becomes my power. His pain becomes my composure.

As I slip down the front of his body, I think about

how far I'm pushing him into places he doesn't want to go. I control him in these few moments, body, mind, and soul.

As I kneel in front of him, my face is right in front of his beautiful, smooth, long shaft. My mouth is watering as I think about sucking on it. From the way he's breathing, I don't think this manwhore has face-fucked many women. Then it dawns on me— that's not it. He doesn't want me here because of her, because of his wife. This was something she did.

When it's my turn to be the bottom, oh, God— my stomach twists. He's going to go all out. He won't stop, but that's what this is now. I feel calm. His fear empowers me. This isn't edge play. It's far past that, but I don't care.

Leaning in, I hear him gasp as he tries to evade me. I take my hands and place them on his ass, and pull his erection toward my mouth. His muscles are corded tight, trying as hard as he can to pull away, but he can't break the chains.

Leaning in closer, I press his shaft to my cheek and drag the tip across my face, one side and then the other. Sean is barely breathing, but he manages to say my name. It's one cry, one plea to stop. This will break him. It'll break me. "Paige."

The problem is simple. I said I'd help him, and I've never felt like this before. I'm perfectly calm, stronger than I thought possible. I feel like my old self, but better. Why? I don't understand it, but I know that this is a give and take. Right now I'm taking. In a moment, I'll have to give it back to him.

He'll break me, he'll have to. He has to feel this clarity, this sense of control. It's a high that feels unbreakable.

He watches me for a moment, and our eyes meet. If he felt this, he'd know it was worth it.

"Do you still trust me?" I watch him, doubting he'll say yes. This is so wrong, so far outside the norm, even at Club Noir.

Sean nods once. It's a jerky movement followed by a hard swallow that makes his Adam's apple move in his neck. His dark hair is tousled and damp with sweat. His body glistens in the red light.

I lunge forward and take his hard length in my mouth, sucking and sliding my tongue over his shaft as I do so. Sean yells and tries to jerk away, but he can't. Placing my hands on his ass steadies him. His head thrashes as if he doesn't enjoy my mouth on his cock, but it gets bigger and harder as I suck him.

Each pass of my tongue makes him groan between gritted teeth. Every time I push him over the edge makes me more powerful.

I'm greedy and don't take it slowly. I want to taste him. I work him, pressing him with my tongue and forcing him down my throat, taking him exactly the way I want as he bucks against me, swearing as he does so. I feel it coming, too much too fast. He moans and stops fighting me. As he comes, his hips pump against my mouth, pushing deep into my throat. He thrusts between my lips, filling my mouth with come and I swallow, only to be treated to more. I drink him until there's nothing left.

When I stand, I notice the way he's hanging in the chains. His shoulders are slumped like he's defeated. It's only temporary, though, because as soon as I unchain him, he'll find out that this high is perfect.

Before we have a chance to find out, there's the sound of a lock beeping. The door to the hallway is thrown open, and Gabe is standing there with Claire. She squeaks. "I'm sorry, Paige. I thought you were in trouble when you didn't show up on stage."

Gabe looks pissed. "This is not what Club Noir is about. The owner is going to skin you."

Chapter 13

I'm sitting in an office waiting to speak to the infamous Miss Black. It's her club and the guard was beyond pissed. He took Sean before I could say anything else. Claire was afraid something horrible happened to me, and they expected to find things the other way around.

It's going to depend on Sean and what he says to her. We were all put in separate rooms within the club to wait. It's not a matter of being thrown out of the club. I could deal with that. It's Miss Black's reputation with rule breakers. She doesn't take having sex on the premises lightly. She's done things to people, things that makes me feel sick sitting here. She could tip off David, but that would be too direct. She'll wait and do something else, something worse.

Before I have a chance to wonder about anything

else, an older woman with a playmate figure walks into the room. She's probably got ten years on me, and more class than I thought possible. She's wearing a black dress that clings to her figure. Luscious black hair cascades down her back like a sheet of water. Red lips are pulled into an amused smile, which scares the hell out of me. There's something about her that is frightening.

"Miss Driskill, it's a pleasure to finally meet you, although I must say that I'm surprised about the circumstances. I wouldn't expect my best bottom to sexually accost another member." She's the devil's daughter. I'm sure of it. Something about her scares me in a way that's unreal.

Trying to explain, I offer, "I didn't—"

She holds up a hand and looks irritated. "Don't bother attempting to refute it. Mr. Ferro told me everything. It's really too bad since you earned every perk all the way up to Level Nine. Such a shame."

"I didn't break the rules." Technically. Sort of. I wasn't in a playroom. And it wasn't sex, like the vag-shaggers in the hallway. It was a blowjob. I doubt that rationale will go far with this woman. She's already made up her mind. She hates me.

Miss Black walks around to a black glass desk that matches the bar downstairs and sits. She opens her hand and smiles. "Then explain. Why were you in a supply closet with a wealthy man chained to the grate? You knew it wasn't a public area and you knew the rules."

I start rambling, suddenly worried she's going to have that Gabe guy tie me up and drive me away in the trunk of an old Caddy. "We were scheduled to be on stage on Level Four. I went to the prop room looking for something different, and Mr. Ferro followed me. We got locked in."

She nods, not believing me even though that part was mostly true. "Explain why you had sex with him. Please indulge me. Was he good?"

I blink. My mouth opens and shuts. I hesitate. "What? I don't know if he's good, we didn't—"

She cuts me off before I can say anything else. "Please, Paige! He was covered in sweat and chained. What was it going to be for round two?"

"Wait, we never did round one!"

She cocks her head to the side. "Really? You didn't ride his cock so you can go brag to your girlfriends that you fucked a Ferro? Or are you going to sell pictures to the papers? He's already been slaughtered in the press. If you think I'm going to let you-"

I jump up and slap my hands on her desk. "I did not ride him. I am not bragging. And I do not tell anyone that I come here. Ferro had nothing to do with it."

"How dare you!" Miss Black is livid. I don't know what I've said, but she clearly plans to kill me right now. Before she can stab me in the head with her pen, the door opens.

She looks like she may have an aneurism, but that viciousness retracts and she's suddenly all smiles. "Mr. Ferro, I thought we called your car?" She looks confused, as if she expected him to be gone already.

Sean is composed again, but I sense a fragility in him that was absent before. "You did, thank you very much. I realized that I have Miss Driskill's gloves in my car. I gave her a ride here earlier."

"Mr. Ferro." I nod at him, unsure.

"Again, I apologize." Sean's lips form a thin line as he presses them together and lets out a rush of air. His shoulders are perfectly squared and his jaw tenses once more. "Miss Black, I was aware of the rules. I take full responsibility for any infractions, as I said earlier. His eyes cut to me for a second before returning to Miss Black.

"It wasn't a minor infraction, Mr. Ferro. You both know the consequences." Her voice is firm and unforgiving. She folds her delicate arms across her chest and stares him down.

Charm bubbles up from somewhere inside Sean. He takes a step toward her, tipping his head to the side the slightest bit. "I didn't want to waste an evening. Is that so wrong?"

Miss Black's death-lock on her forearms loosens, and she rolls her eyes. "You're both on probation until further notice."

MANWHORE

A smile spreads across Sean's lips as he tucks his hands into his pockets and steps toward Miss Black. He leans in close to her ear and says something so softly I can't hear it. He lingers there for a moment before pulling away. "Think about it."

Whatever he said to Miss Black shocked her, because the woman is standing there with her lips parted unable to speak. Her perfectly shaped brows are high on her face, and her hands fall to her sides.

"Miss Driskill, if you'll follow me."

Chapter 14

Before I can say anything, we're out the door.

I'm on his heels when the elevator door slides open. He pushes me inside, even though I'm trying to get back into that office. "Sean, stop. I need to go back."

He laughs and shakes his head. "That's the worst thing you can do."

"But she has my collar! Do you know what I had to do to earn that? I can't leave it there." I feel sick. As the elevator descends to the ground floor, it's clear that I've lost it.

Sean is leaning against the wall of the elevator. When we are about to reach the ground level, his arm juts forward and pulls the emergency stop. The little room buzzes and then goes dark before a red light illuminates the tiny space.

Before I can ask what he's doing, his body presses mine against the wall. His breath is in my ear. "What you did up there was off limits. It was out of line." He's angry. His words come out in a rush with a decent amount of force for a whisper.

The way he's behaving makes my pulse race. The hairs on the back of my neck rise on end and a hollow spot forms in the center of my chest. I manage to keep the fear out of my voice, barely. "It was what you needed."

"No, it wasn't. It didn't help. It didn't free me. If anything, you shoved me face-first into the memory that I wanted to forget."

"I know." I turn my face away from him. I can't help it. He can't know, but at that moment he seems to sense it.

"You know? What the fuck does that mean?"

I'm trying so hard to stay still, but my arms are starting to shake. I feel the sensation snaking its way up from my fingers. Soon it'll choke my voice and force tears from my eyes. He presses his chest against me harder. His hands jerk to my cheeks, turning my face toward his—to meet those eyes that turned to ice. He can feel my tremor beneath his hand, but he doesn't release me.

"We're the same—"

He cuts me off. "No, we are not."

"Fine, pretend that you're okay, but I'm done pretending, and if you'd listen to me for half a second, you'd be done, too." His grip loosens, but he doesn't step away.

"Explain." It's a single word command.

I swallow hard and give the explanation that's been forming in my mind since we were caught. "Most people who enjoy edge play like the thrill of it—they want to be commanded and pushed right up to the edge. But for people like us, that does nothing, unless you're the top. Unless you push the bottom just past the edge, a fraction of an inch past their breaking point."

Sean releases me and steps back. He stares, shocked. "You knew what you were doing?"

I nod. "Edge play can be fatal if you do things that endanger the bottom's life, but what if you found their worst fear and pressed it? Most people have a breaking point, but their caution flags shoot up way before they reach the cliff. What if you were to take them to the edge of that precipice and dangle them over the edge?"

Sean stands there breathing hard, eyes wide and darkening by the moment. It's as if he's fighting my suggestion, even though he sees the allure. Without a word, he smacks the button that brings the elevator to life again. His eyes look me over once, and then again.

When the doors slide open, Gabe frowns at us and I hurry past. Sean walks in long strides, his long black coat billowing behind him like some kind of supervillain. I rush up beside him and follow him out of the club and toward his car. It's waiting next to the curb. The driver rushes around to open the door, but Sean remains next to me. It's late now, and the sidewalks are mostly empty. Many of the grates are closed across the front of the stores that line the streets. A store owner a few doors down is washing off the section of cement in front of his store with a hose.

I wrap my arms around my middle and shiver. My coat is still inside, and I'm standing in public wearing next to nothing. Sean doesn't offer me a ride. He doesn't say to climb into the car. He just watches me.

I want to yell at him, but I reign in my temper and find some composure. "Maybe I shouldn't have done it. The thing is, while it was happening, I didn't feel that dread anymore. The pain lifted, and I felt like I could control my life once more. That unsettling feeling vanished. For a moment, I was safe."

"I understand why you did it, but you crossed a line, Miss Driskill." Sean notices me shivering and rubbing my hands over my arms. He seems aggravated, but he shucks his jacket and drapes it over my shoulders.

"I don't need it." I pull the coat off and try to shove it back, but he won't take it.

"You have enough issues without your boss

seeing you here with me. Add in that outfit and it'll be clear that your code of ethics is rather questionable. Put the jacket on."

He's right, so I stop fighting him. I jam my fist through one sleeve and then the other. I wrap the fabric tightly around in front and fold my arms over my chest to hold it closed. "Maybe I should apologize, but I can't. Sean, if I let you do it to me— you'd see what I'm talking about."

His gaze narrows, and he steps into my space. His lips curl as if he's disgusted. "I don't want to see. I'd rather not know what it feels like to rip someone to shreds and then get off on it. That's not playing, Miss Driskill. It's an attribute that needs psychological help."

"You don't think I've tried?" I'm in his face, spewing things that I've never said to anyone. "You don't think I've gone to counseling, tried therapy, prescriptions, and anything else that could possibly help me to deal with what happened to me? Nothing else works! And you know that because you're dealing with the same thing."

"Normal people place parameters on behavior and what you're suggesting exceeds that by far!"

"Normal people don't have to deal with the lots we were handed. Normal people can say what's moral, because their survival isn't filled with bloody deaths that never stop screaming. When they go to sleep at night, they worry about work, money, family, and things that we would love to be freaking out over. We don't sleep. There is no silence for us—no peace. When things slow down, we hear their voices and pleas, and it makes no fucking difference because we can't change the past. We both stood there, useless. We take no pleasure in anything, and I'm not even sure I remember what pleasure feels like. I haven't felt anything but fear and grief for so long. It's every day and it never stops. There's no way around it, so the only path left is to walk right through it and hope to God that there's something on the other side. But you know what? There is no other side. I've been walking for years and there's nothing. I'm trapped, stuck in the middle of a nightmare that never ends. I can't wake up, I can't change it, and I can't escape. That's how we're the same—we've died, but we're not dead—we're stuck here living a hellish existence with no way out. So, how can we possibly fall into their set of rules?"

He shakes his head. "I'm sorry. Maybe you think I'm a monster, but I'm not doing that to you, Paige. I'm not getting off by torturing you. I know what happened to you—why you're like this. I know that you're trying to forget what happened to your mother. I know what you fear the most."

I can't swallow. My mouth is dry and my jaw is locked. I stand there in front of him, feeling like shit. I want to cry, but I can't. I have no tears. "Don't judge me too harshly, Sean. There will come a time when you can't stand it anymore, and when that time comes, you know where I am. I won't condemn you for it. It's just the way it is for people like us. We're not monsters, but we've seen things that are so dark no amount of light makes them better. Do what you need to do to ease your conscience, but you're going to face this sooner or later."

"No, I won't."

Chapter 15

I'd rather stab myself in the face with a fork than sit in court the next day. I'm exhausted, and I don't want to see Sean. I'm nervous he's going to say something about the club or the other night, but he doesn't even look at me.

Days pass, curiosity gets the better of me, and I find myself snooping around Club Noir. I can't go upstairs without my collar, and Gabe will snitch to his boss if he sees me, so I wear my hair down, letting it become a brown sheet that covers half my face. I stopped at Sephora on the way over and told them to make me look like a picture I found on Pinterest. Forty-five minutes later, I'm wearing enough makeup that even David wouldn't recognize me. Since he's totally anal, that's saying something.

I sit at the sleek black bar and sip my drink. The

evening crowd trickles in slowly and the place is bursting at the seams by midnight. There's no sign of Ferro. Probation or not, I was sure he'd show.

I down my last drink and stand, straightening my skirt and tucking my long hair behind my ear before heading outside. The night air is freezing. My jacket is MIA, but I still have Sean's soft wool coat. I tug up the collar and push through the front door.

My gaze is on the sidewalk, noticing the splotches of water that fall from the sky. It's raining. I step toward the curb with the intention of hailing a cab when a black Bentley pulls up in front of me. The window slides down part way. Sean sits inside concealed in shadows.

"Are you looking for trouble, Miss Driskill?" His voice is flat, lifeless. It's as if with every passing day, there's less and less of him.

"It depends. Are you trouble, Mr. Ferro?" I lean in toward the window and catch his eyes. They're vacant, hollow

He ignores the question. Instead, he lets his eyes sweep over me before saying, "Nice coat."

I smirk and straighten. Pulling at the lapel, I twirl to show it off. "It is, actually, very warm and soft." He doesn't smile. I get serious. "Actually I came here to give it back to you."

"Lies don't become you, Miss Driskill." The raindrops grow bigger until it's pouring. I start to pull my arms out of the long coat, getting ready to shove it through the window when he suddenly opens the door. "Come inside, and keep the coat. I wouldn't want to win this court case because Cunning lost his prodigy."

Shocked, I stand there for a moment. Water pours off my hair and drips into my eyes and mouth. He thinks I'm smart? The man who believes he's smarter than God said I'm a prodigy.

"Don't look so shocked, Paige. We both know what you are."

That sounds like an insult. "What would that be, Sean?" I step toward the car, drenched, with his coat hanging over my arm.

"You're willing to do whatever it takes to survive, to win, to live. It's a trait that doesn't remain neatly in the center of a compartment in your mind. It affects everything you do. Even right now, you're trying to discern whether or not to accept a ride. You know you can't find a cab."

"Actually, I'm trying to decide why you're following me. You said I was a deviant, and you wouldn't ever do what I did, yet here you are. Did you change your mind?" I place my hand on the roof of the car as I speak, leaning in close enough to drip on his designer suit.

His jaw tightens at the suggestion, and those dark lashes lower to the pavement. When he looks into my face once more, there's a plastic smile on his mouth. "Far from it. I realized I have a piece of trash, and I'm trying to decide how to part with it." He reaches down and lifts something off the seat next to him. The gems catch my eye, and I realize it's my collar. The band twists and I can see the embossing on the inside of the leather: PAIGE DRISKILL ~ CLUB NOIR.

Don't react. I chant the words over and over again to prevent myself from lunging for the collar. I remain in place, dripping on a billionaire, and getting wetter by the moment.

He twists the band between his fingers and looks at it. "The fact that I know you're smart isn't the issue here. No, my thought is singular. The question is, can David Cunning win my case without you? My thoughts on the matter are clear." He smirks, and those eyes connect with mine, making my stomach plummet to the pavement. "It would be a shame if this were to turn up at your office."

I work my jaw and let out a crazy sounding laugh. "What do you want?"

Sean steps out of the car, into the rain. His dark hair is instantly wet and hanging in his eyes. He leans in, close enough to touch without touching, and speaks next to my ear. "When I decide, I'll let you know." He pulls back a little bit and looks at me. It's as if he wants to say something, but he's conflicted.

There's a war raging inside of him. I can see it. His walls are thick and hardening. Sean Ferro will be a devastatingly ruthless man when this is over. The worst part is that I'm the one who made it happen.

When he speaks again, his voice is softer. "I'll be in touch." The last word purses his lips so that they nearly touch mine. In the cold rain, I can sense his warm lips. I almost lean in, but I'm afraid.

What have I done?

Chapter 16

The trial drags on and every day my stomach is in knots waiting for him to expose me. David is the king of black and white. There is no room for anything like Club Noir in his office. No explanation could make him understand, so I remain silent, waiting.

Sean's demeanor becomes colder in court. I don't even need to draw attention to it anymore. He's becoming the monster I painted him to be—sitting there stoic and calloused. When we show pictures of his dead wife, he doesn't cry, look away, or show any signs of remorse. David uses Sean's apathy, drawing attention to it. He's not the only one. The press is there every day, and they never give up.

Sean has a never-ending stream of people who swear at him and curse him as he comes down the steps of the courthouse every day. Tonight, I remain on the top steps watching him descend. They hurl insults along with malicious words. New Yorkers aren't kind people to begin with, and Sean has crawled under their skin. They think he's a killer, that he brutally murdered his pregnant wife and called 911 while laughing about it. I may have leaked that part. It was the nail in the coffin of his public perception.

As Sean's feet shuffle down the steps, he stops. David is speaking to a reporter and can't turn to look, but I can. An older man yells at him, his reddened face haggard as he yells. Sean's spine is straight, and he doesn't flinch. He stands there taking the verbal assault. His jaw is locked, almost defiantly so. His hands hang by his sides, and his fingers rest against his suit pants. The hand closest to me, the hand that's turned away from the crowd, presses into his leg for a moment. It's the only sign this man has affected Sean in any way.

When I get home later, I push the door open and stand on the threshold. Jess is belting out Abba at the top of her lungs while dancing around the apartment with headphones on. Her eyes are closed, and she's a dancing queen. I wish I could forget reality that easily. Maybe I need more Abba.

Or maybe not. I close the door and stand in the hallway staring at the knob. My life is a black hole. It sucks everything to oblivion. I'm so turned around I no longer know what to do. It's almost midnight. I've been shuffling through files and looking at papers for David all night. I'm seeing double and ready to pass out.

I press my back against the wall and slide down to the floor. I stick my feet out in front of me and kick off my heels. I watch at the stairwell for a while, not thinking anything until two feet stop in front of me. Shiny expensive shoes by that new guy—I'm blanking on his name. When I glance up, I nearly choke. "Sean?"

He stands there, still wearing his suit from court. His dark hair is hanging in his eyes like he was pulling at it for hours. The dark circles under his eyes that have grown too big to go unnoticed. His hands are by his sides. He flexes his fingers once, then twice, and clears his throat before he speaks. "I've changed my mind."

Chapter 17

I'm still sitting on the floor, legs crossed at the ankles, and looking up at him. "I'm sorry, what was that?"

Jess belts out from behind the door, "I'm the dancing quee-bfff!" There's a series of thuds as she falls to the floor. I pinch the bridge of my nose and try not to laugh. I'd ask if she's okay, but she's already singing again and jumping around the room.

The guy below us is banging on the ceiling and yelling, "Shut the fuck up!"

I look up at Sean with tired eyes and take a deep breath before pushing my hair out of my face. "Listen, I'm no longer interested. As you can see, I need to keep my roommate from getting evicted for being young, free, and way older than seventeen. I'm living with the dancing queen. She's kind of a pain in the ass, and I'm not in an Abba mood or I'd be on the other side of the door."

Sean presses his lips together as if he's trying not to laugh. "I can see that."

I give him a look. "Bite me."

"I already offered. You said you'd rather help out your friend. Have a good night." He turns and heads for the stairs.

Before he's down the first step, I call out, "Who was that man?"

He stops and looks over at me. "Amanda's father." There's no further explanation. He just turns and vanishes down the staircase.

"Wait, what?" I scurry to my feet, scooping up my shoes and bag, before rushing after him. "Sean, hang on a second." I'm a flight above him and see his dark head bobbing down the flight below. One more and he's out the door.

No wonder why he came looking for me tonight. His own father-in-law publicly accused him of murder. I slip as I round the landing and catch myself before I fall on my butt. I make a weird strangled sound before I right myself. Sean stops and looks up. He stands perfectly still, and those bright blue eyes look up at me. His lips are parted the tiniest amount as if he wants to speak. His strong hands grip the banister harder making his fingertips turn red. He closes his eyes and turns his face to the side for a moment, working his jaw. When he opens those dark lashes, he drops his hand from the railing and continues down the staircase.

"Sean!" I call after him and fly down the stairs, but he's too far ahead of me.

He disappears through the door before I reach the ground floor. Panting, I shove out the glass door and onto the sidewalk. My stockings cling to the pavement as I take a few steps in each direction, trying to see where he went. There are too many people, even now. New York never sleeps. It's always running, always bustling. Yellow cabs blur by as the sound of the city fills my head. I walk down the block and try to see if he's on foot, but Sean probably ducked into his car and took off.

Today was one of the worst days of his life. Tomorrow won't be better. Sean knows that. It's why he was here, and I turned him away. I press my fingers to my forehead to ward off a headache and dip my head.

A hand touches my shoulder lightly and jerks me from my thoughts. I scream like a crazy woman and round on my assailant with my heels aimed at his face. A strong arm juts up and blocks me before my heel connects with his temple. Breathing hard, I stand there staring into Sean's face.

He opens his mouth and then shuts it again. He does it several times before he says, "I can't go home. I can't. Not today. Not ever again. If I walk away from this, I'm leaving New York. I'll never come back."

I watch his lips move and notice that he's pulled his tie loose from around his neck. Stubble dusts his normally clean-shaven face, and his eyes look weary. I nod and lower my gaze to the sidewalk. "I can understand that."

"Come with me. Tell me what you know—how you live with it. You started to, and I told you to stop. I judged you when I should have been listening." He's watching me so intently that the pit of my stomach drops.

Just then, a woman walks by and spits on Sean. She keeps walking and screams, "Monster!"

Sean removes his handkerchief from his breast pocket and wipes it away. He doesn't seem phased, but I know he isn't unaffected. "Don't pity me."

"I don't. I agreed with her at one point."

"And now—?"

Inhaling sharply, I blurt out the thoughts I've wanted to say for so long. "Now I wonder what I would have done if they'd said I'd killed my mother. I wonder how I would have survived if they thought my hands were covered in her blood because I hurt her, if they hadn't realized I tried to help even though it was too late. Now I realize what I've done. There's only one monster standing here, Sean, and it isn't you."

His castle keep is built, and sealed. There's no light in his eyes, not anymore. Sean holds out his hand. "There's a hotel not too far from here. Come with me."

Chapter 18

I remain in the bar until Sean finishes checking into a room, and then meet him there. No one can see us together. I have something he needs, I'm just not certain I want him to try it out on me. Once Sean understands what I'm about to tell him, he will be truly frightening.

I raise my hand to knock on the door, but it swings open before I make a sound. Sean is standing there in his dark pants and a white dress shirt unbuttoned at the neck, the tie long removed. One hand holds a crystal glass with amber liquid while the other holds the door open. "Come in."

I pass under his arm, wishing my racing heart would slow down. My palms are sweaty, and I can't swallow. Nervously, I glance around the room. It's large, with a big four-poster bed overlooking the city from behind wraparound picture windows and a little balcony. There's an enormous white marble bathroom off the bedroom with a tub and a separate shower.

I pull off my heels and pad over to the windows in my ripped stockings. The city always looks so peaceful from up high. I press my fingers against the cold glass and look down.

I feel Sean behind me. His presence is unmistakable because it's both alluring and frightening at the same time. "Tell me what to do."

I turn and look up at him. His body is tense, with every muscle corded tight. "I can't. It doesn't work that way, Sean. You have to find it—something that makes you feel free and in control. It's not going to be something we've already done, or you'd know. It's going to be something different every time, something I wouldn't want to face in the daylight, never mind at night."

"Explain." He sets the glass down on top of the bar, and then walks over to me. He takes my hands and pulls me toward the bed.

I move slowly, one foot and then the other. "I don't know how it works, but when I was with you the other day—it was like that. It freed me for a while. It's almost as if your fear fed my peace."

"It's a parasite relationship." He rubs his thumbs over the back of my hands, down by my wrists. He glances up at me from under his lashes, wanting to hear more.

"In some ways, yes, I guess it is. What I did to you—it was something you didn't want. If you hadn't been chained, what would you have done?"

He blinks and drops my hands, ready to step away, but I reach out and take hold of his wrists. "You know, so tell me. You had a clear thought—something that wasn't kosher."

He pulls away and turns his back on me. "It was far past kosher, farther from sane than anything I've ever thought before. It was an image, something that I couldn't do to anyone, especially not you."

"Why?"

"Because it's cruel." He looks over his shoulder and swallows hard. Those eyes that have been so cold and unfeeling fill with an unreadable emotion.

"What I did to you was cruel. I stole something from you—something you intended to keep for her—right?"

He turns toward me and nods. "What you did was not fucking, what you did was sex—and sex is like food, it's a necessity of life. You destroyed an act I wanted to keep pure." Anger seeps into his voice, and he does little to hide it.

"I wanted it, so I took it. That's the way this works. It requires more trust than anything else. I'm giving you permission to take me to the edge and hold me over the side—just don't drop me. That's the only rule. Don't push me so far I can't come back." I touch his arm and look up at him.

He pulls away and shakes his head. "I can't. It's too much. It's over the line, a line I don't want to cross." His voice fades on the last words.

I walk up behind him and speak carefully. My hands hover over his back. "It's something you need to do, something you want, or you wouldn't have come looking for me. You don't need a fuckbuddy, Sean. You need someone who can both dish it out and take it. You need me." I rest my hands on his shoulders and trail my finger along the back of his neck, knowing he'll hate it.

Sean rounds on me faster than expected and shirks me off. "Don't."

"Do it." I step closer to him.

Sean shakes his head and backs up. "No. Let me think."

"There's nothing to think about. It's an instinct. Act on it. Do it." I reach for him again, trying to bait him. I touch his cheek, tracing my finger along his jaw before his hand grips mine hard and throws me off.

Sean sits down on the bed, grabs his head in his hands, and pulls at his hair. "I can't accept this. I shouldn't have come here." His voice is barely audible. He runs his hands through his dark hair a few more times before gritting his teeth and shaking his head.

He's fighting his moral compass. It's telling him

not to cross this line. Maybe I should listen. Maybe I should leave, but I feel I owe him this. Before I know what I'm saying, I tell him, "It was me. I'm the one who suggested you're a monster. It was my idea to make people think you were laughing when you called 911. The woman who spit on you today—I can take credit for that. Everyone hates you because of me. It wasn't David or anyone else. I took this case because I wanted everyone to hate you as much as I did."

As I speak, he continues to hold his head in his hands, but he doesn't move. He doesn't breathe. A moment of silence passes between us and when Sean stands I'm truly afraid. The way he looks at me makes my body react. My fight or flight instinct kicks in and my feet want to run, but I lock my knees in place.

"You did that? You were the one who told those lies?" His eyes narrow to thin slits and I know I've given him enough reasons to leave his morals behind.

"Yes." I say it proudly and smile at him. "All of it was my idea, and whatever you want to do now, I'm saying yes. Cane me, whip me, tie me up and use me. Do whatever it is you imagined."

Sean leans in close to my ear and grabs the hair at the nape of my neck. He jerks my head back and hisses in my ear. "I'm going to take you to the edge and hold you there until you scream for me to stop, but I won't. That's what you've done to me with your lies. You wanted a monster, Miss Driskill—well, here he is."

It's part of the game, part of the play. I know it is, but I'm shaking so hard I can't stop. I try to pull away, but he won't let me. Before I can scream, Sean twists me around, ripping off my blouse and tearing the fabric as he goes. He takes it in his hands and tears it down the middle, twice, making one strip of cloth and then another. Gasping, I stand frozen, watching. He reaches for me again and rips off my skirt, and tosses it aside. I'm left standing in a pair of white undies and a nude colored bra.

He looks at me, his eyes seeing something else, something to come. He rips off my bra and then while I'm still screaming from that, he grabs my panties with both hands, tearing them off my body.

No. Oh, God, no! Trembling, I back away from him. I know what he's doing, and I'm panicking—I can't submit to what he wants. Hands up, palms toward him, I shake my head and plead. "Please, don't. Not this."

He doesn't listen, nor does he stop. He takes my wrists and pulls them behind my back, tying them together with the scraps from my panties. After that, he pushes me down on the bed, face-first, holding me there until I can barely breathe. When he pulls my hair, my head tips back and my mouth hangs wide open, gasping for air. Suddenly a strip of cloth—my shirt—is gagging me. He stuffs the fabric into my mouth then ties a second layer across it and behind my head.

Every movement is executed precisely—as if he'd been there, as if he'd seen the files of how my mother was raped and stabbed. They used her clothes to tie her up and gag her. They forced her onto the bed, and then dragged her onto the floor in the kitchen and stabbed her in the side after drawing on her arms and legs with the tip of the blade.

He can't. I pull at my bindings, but they're becoming tighter. My wrists ache, and I struggle to breathe. He holds me on the bed, leaning on my back, as I fight against him, but there's no point. He's too strong.

When I feel the cold cloth around my ankles, I lose it. I try to kick, feeling my mind slip too far into panic. My heart is ready to burst through my chest, and my mind can't process that this is real. I feel something within me wither and back away. It slips from place, like a fallen ribbon.

Sean pushes me to the floor and binds my feet behind my back. They raped her before they did this. Sean didn't rape me. He didn't touch me like that, but the rest is the same, accurate. Using my clothes, ripping them, throwing me on the floor and tying me like this. Everything is identical, except the rape. My face presses against the carpet, and I'm helpless. I lay on my belly, tied up like an animal. Sean walks past me and turns off the lights one by one, plummeting us into darkness.

The weight of my body in this position makes my breasts ache. I never lay like this; I never want to remember that night. Now I'm reliving it in a way I never imagined. Tears roll down my cheeks as I wait for the next part. I wonder if he'll cut me, if he's lost his mind. When I feel the cold steel on my leg, I scream into the gag. I try to pull away, but I'm bound too tightly. I feel the cold cuts of a blade, one by one, followed by a warm drip of blood. He does one leg and then the next, marking me with the same symbols, the same words. When he straddles my back, I already know what he's going to carve into my skin. WHORE. It was there on my mother.

The long lines of the W cutting into my skin are too much. I buck and try to roll over, but he doesn't let me. Sean presses me down with one hand while he cuts me with the other.

When he finishes, he grabs hold of my ankles and pulls me across the room. The carpet burns my breasts, but I'm no longer screaming. I've retreated to the back of my mind, to a place filled with buzzing silence, where I can't feel what he's doing to me. It's a place where it doesn't matter.

I'm limp when he drags me into the bathroom. The cold marble doesn't register, even though it's pressing against my breasts and stomach. My cheek is pressed to the floor as he walks away. I'm left like that, lying in a pool of warm blood on the cold floor.

This is how I found her. This is what I saw when I ran inside that day. I cut her free and watched her pale hand fall limply into a puddle of blood. The movement in my mind is suddenly real. My wrists fall freely to the floor, and someone is rolling me over. I don't struggle. I don't fight.

I see Sean looking down at me as he bends over to lift me up into his arms. He carries me over to the bed and places me on the white sheets. He reaches for the remnants of the ankle restraints and pulls them away. He spreads my legs and unzips his pants. I'm aware of him, but I no longer care. I'm here, but I'm not.

The gag remains. He takes my hands and places them above my head and leans in closely, and kisses my breasts. I feel him pressing against my core as he shifts, pressing his body to mine. He moves and rocks into me gently. He holds my hips in his hands and pushes into me slowly. His sapphire eyes lock on my face as he does it. He fills me, pushing in deep, over and over again. He doesn't speak as he does it. There are no false words—only the sound of his breathing becoming more and more jagged.

His hands cup my ass as the rhythmic rocking turns frantic. He pushes in harder and faster, until that last time where he slams into me as deep as possible and arches his back. His eyes close and he stays like that for a moment before his shoulders sag, and he collapses on top of me.

He rolls off of me, and I feel my mind slowly turning over, wondering how long it will take for me to die. I don't move when he gets up and turns on the shower. I assumed I'd be too weak. I blink and wonder why it feels like I'm waking up. I wiggle my toes and am surprised when they move. I sit up, shocked that I can. I pull the gag from my mouth and touch my arms. They're wet, but when I pull my hand away, there's no blood. It's too dark in here. I can't see what he did to me.

I slip out of bed, and pad to the bathroom. The lights are bright and blur my vision. I blink and rub my eyes as I walk over to the mirror. I expect to see my body covered in cuts and blood pouring down my arms, but when I wipe my hand across the glass— there's nothing there. No blood. No cuts.

I glance down at my legs and see it's the same. Sean is in the shower. I walk over and pull the door open. I feel half alive. It's like he sucked every last drop of sanity and hope from my entire body.

He smiles at me awkwardly and holds out his hand. "Come in."

I shake my head, instinctively backing away. "What did you do to me? I thought there was a knife. I felt the cuts and the blood." My voice is shaking, and it's not until then that I realize my entire body is shaking.

Sean holds out his hand, palms up. "Touch my

hand, Paige. Do it. What you're feeling will fade the more you touch things and people."

I don't believe him, but I feel too weird. I reach out and touch the pad of his finger. The normal simmering spark between us amplifies, feeling like licking a light socket. The charge rushes through me, enough that I gasp and pull away.

Sean lowers his hand and explains. "That happened to me, too, after you did that to me."

"I did not do this to you."

"Yes, you did. You made me relive something that pushed me too far. You didn't break me, but it came close. I did the same thing to you." I can't read his thoughts or tell if he has any remorse. I'm not sure if I care.

My arms are over my breasts even though my bottom is bare. I feel fragile like I might come unglued. "I felt the knife. I felt blood."

"It was warm oil and a letter opener, Paige."

I stand there, thinking, still unable to believe it even though both objects are on the counter. Before I can say anything else, he steps out of the shower, naked and dripping. He walks over to me and stops before touching me. Water beads on his hair and drips from his chin. "Thank you. I haven't felt like this in a long time. I owe you, Paige."

"No, you don't. I did this to you. I caused your suffering to be more than anyone could possibly bear. The worst part is I know you didn't do it. I just don't understand why you aren't trying to kill the person who did. Amanda's killer is still walking around."

He shakes his head and averts his eyes. "That person won't kill anyone again."

My eyebrow jumps into my hairline. "You can't tell me things like that. I have to report it."

He steps closer, his naked body barely touching mine and I'm such a freak because I want to jump him. He shakes his head. "You asked a question. That's the answer. Amanda's killer is gone. There's nothing to report or call."

His hands are on mine, and I'm not sure if I did it or he did. "You didn't do it?"

He shakes his head. "No." His voice is soft.

"I believe you."

Sean touches my face and wipes the tear stains off my face with his thumb. "Let me help you feel a little bit better, if you trust me."

I feel a smile take hold of my mouth as I nod. "A girl's got to eat."

"True." Sean's mouth comes down on mine, and he kisses me softly.

Chapter 19

The trial ended a few weeks ago, and Sean Ferro is no longer the heir to a massive fortune because he walked away from it. That made my jaw drop, but he did it. He took the first plane out of New York and hasn't looked back.

Sean did something with me that plummeted my mind into darkness and then brought me back to life. It was frightening and glorious. I've never forgotten him because of it.

It's early spring, and daffodils are popping up in Central Park. I've gotten back into the habit of jogging, and I value that time in the morning more than anything else. Since my night with Sean, the mental barricade I was afraid to acknowledge is no longer there. I no longer need Club Noir, and have no intention of ever going back.

I shower and dress before Jess falls out of bed and heads to her yoga class. I spend the day crushing bad guys and wishing I had someone to share my nights. I'm not exactly lonely. I just know there's someone out there for me, and I haven't bothered to look for him.

When I get home that night, Jess has a bucket of chicken. I smile at her and plop down on our couch.

Jess hands it to me. "Your favorite, right?"

I take the bucket, thinking it's filled with fried chicken and glance inside. Buttermilk biscuits. I grin at her. "Oh, my, God! How'd you know?" I pop a piece of bread in my mouth and savor the flavor. I swear it's like these are deep fried angels or something—they taste like heaven in my mouth.

"Well, you've been working too hard and running too much." She sips her huge-o bottle of water and lifts a chicken leg to her mouth.

"You're a yoga teacher!"

"And I'm eating fried chicken and our living room isn't Feng Shui enough. I know. My aura is totally out of whack. It's throwing me off. By the way, this came for you today. I found it stuffed in the mailbox."

She tosses me a beat up padded envelope. I put down my food, rip it open, and look inside. A smile creeps across my face as I recognize the black leather collar with nine stones.

There's a note enclosed:

Paige,
I thought you might need this. If
you're ever in California, look me up.
-S.F.

He sent it back. It means I no longer need to worry about this suddenly showing up and ruining my career.

"What is it?" Jess asks.

"Just junk mail. Nothing important." Not anymore. I get off the couch, pad across the apartment into the kitchen, and open the garbage pail.

I toss the package in the trash with no regrets. That part of my life is over and I'm glad. I finally understand how people get over Club Noir and move on from the dark places in their past. I'm finally there. I'm ready to start looking for Mr. Right.

* * *

The End

* * *

To ensure you don't miss H.M. Ward's next book, text HMWARD (one word) to 24587 to receive a text reminder on release day.

WANT TO READ MORE ABOUT
SEAN FERRO?

Turn the page to enjoy a **FREE** excerpt of
THE ARRANGEMENT

THE ARRANGEMENT, Vol. 1
by H.M. Ward

Chapter 1

The night air is frigid. It doesn't help that I'm stuck wearing this little black dress in my crap car. I shiver as I try to keep the engine running at a red light. My little battered car is from two decades ago and stalls if I don't rev the engine while I have my foot on the brake. I'm driving with two feet, in a car that's supposed to be an automatic. The heater doesn't work. If I try to turn it on, I'll get my face blasted with white smoke. It's awesome, in an utterly humbling kind of way. At least the car is mine. It gets me where I need to go, most of the time.

The light flips to green and I botch it. I don't gas the car enough and it shudders and stalls. I grumble and grab for the can of ether. The cars behind me blare their horns.

I ignore them. They can go around me. I grab the

can on the seat next to me, kick open my door, and walk around to the hood. I shake the can and spray it into the engine intake. The car will start up as soon as I turn the key now, and I can drive away in shame.

The night air is crisp and filled with exhaust. This road is always busy. It doesn't matter what time of day it is. Angry drivers move around me. Everyone is always in a hurry. It's part of the New York frame of mind. I'm treated to a catcall as a car full of guys blows past me. I flip them the bird and hear their laughter echo as they fade from sight.

Tonight couldn't possibly get any worse. I put the cap on the can of ether. Then it happens. My night takes a one-eighty straight into suckage.

As I drop the hood, it slams shut, and I look through the windshield. "Seriously?" I say at the guy who jumps in my seat. He's wearing a once-blue fluffy coat and hasn't shaved for weeks. He turns the key and my crappy car roars to life. He gasses it and takes off, swerving around me. I stand in the lane staring after him. What a moron. Who'd steal that piece of trash?

Still, it's my car and I need it. After the night I had, I don't want to run after him, but I have to. I need that car. I take off at a full run. My lungs start to burn as I suck in frozen air and exhaust. I run down the shoulder, avoiding trash that's laying in the gutter. My attention is singularly focused on my car. I push my body harder and feel my muscles protest, but I don't hold back. He's getting away.

I manage to run a block when a guy on a motorcycle slows next to me. "That guy stole your car." He sounds shocked.

I can't see his face through the black helmet. It has a tinted visor that covers his face. "No shit, Sherlock," I huff and keep running. My purse is in the car, my only pair of work-acceptable heels, my books—awh, fuck—my books. I paid over a grand for those. They're worth more than the car. I run faster. My dress flares around my thighs as my Chucks help me sprint forward. My body doesn't want to do it. The stitch in my side feels like it's going to bust open.

The guy on the bike is annoying. He rolls next to me and flips up his face shield. I glance at him, wondering what he's doing. Biker guy looks at me like I'm crazy. "Are you trying to catch him?"

"Yes," pointing ahead, huffing. There are three lights on this stretch of road before the ramp to get on the parkway. If he hits a red light, the car will stall and I'll get it back. My lungs are burning and it's not like I have time to explain this. My car has already passed the first light. "If he stops, the car will stall."

"You want me to help?" he glances at the car and then back at me.

I stop and nearly double over. Holy hell, I'm out of shape. I nod and throw my leg over the back of his bike, flashing the cars driving past us. I so don't care. Wrapping my arms around his waist, I hold on tight and say, "Go."

"I was going to call the cops, but this works, too." He sounds amused. I hold onto his trim waist and plaster myself against his back. He's wearing a leather jacket, and I can feel his toned body through the supple material. He pulls into traffic and zips through the lanes. The wind blasts my hair and plasters my eyelashes wide open. We bob and weave, getting closer and closer to my car. My heart is racing so fast that it's going to explode.

I see my car. It's passing the second light. Motorcycle man punches it, and the bike flies under the second intersection just as the light changes. I manage not to shriek. My skirt flies up to my hips, but I don't let go of the biker's waist to push the fabric back down.

We're nearly there when the thief catches the third light. The car in front of him stops, forcing the carjacker to stop as well. As soon as he takes his foot off the gas, my car convulses and white smoke shoots out the tailpipe. The engine ceases. The driver's side door is kicked open and the guy runs.

Motorcycle man pulls up next to my car. I slip off the back of the bike, my heart beating a mile a minute. I can't afford to lose this stuff. I'm barely making it as it is. I look at my car. Everything is still there. I turn back to the guy on the bike as I smooth my skirt back into place.

Tucking my hair behind my ear, I say, "Thanks." I must seem insane.

He flips his face shield up and says, "No problem. Does your car always do that?" A pair of blue eyes meet mine and the floor of my stomach gives way. Damn, he's cute. No, not cute—he's hot.

"Get jacked? No, not always."

He smiles. There's a dusting of stubble on his cheeks. I can barely see it because of the helmet. He raises an eyebrow at me and asks, "This has happened before, hasn't it?"

More times than you'd think. Criminals are really stupid. "Let's just say, this isn't the first time I had to chase after the car. So far no one's made it to the parkway. That damn light takes forever and I keep stalling out in the same spot. You'd think I'd figure it out by now, but…" But I'm mentally challenged and prefer to chase after car thieves. I stop talking and press my lips together. His eyes run over my dress and pause on my sneakers, before returning to my face. Great, he thinks I'm mental.

Turning to the car, I grab another can of ether from the backseat and walk around to the front. I dropped the last can somewhere behind me. I pop the hood and spray. I'm so cold that I've gone numb. As I walk back to my door, I shake my head saying, "Who steals a car that barely runs?"

"Do you need any help?" The guy holds my gaze

for a moment and my stomach twists. He seems sincere, which kills me. A strange compulsion to spill my guts tries to overtake me, but I bash it back down.

Pressing my lips together, I shake my head, and swallow the lump in my throat. Today sucked. I'm totally alone. No one helps me, and yet this guy did. "No, I'm okay," I lie as I slip into my car and yank the door shut. "Thanks for the ride." I turn the engine over and smile at him. The window is down. It doesn't go up.

"Anytime." He nods at me, like he wants to say something else. All I can see of his face is his crystal blue eyes and a beautiful mouth. He's sitting on a bike that cost more than my tuition. He's loaded and I've got nothing. A pang of remorse shoots through me, but I need to go. The haves and the have-nots weren't made to mingle. I already learned that lesson once. I don't need to learn it again.

"Thanks," I say before he can ask my name. "I'll see you around." I smile at him and drive away, holding back tears that are building behind my eyes.

It's weird. There are so many shitty people in the world, and on the worst day of my life, I finally find a nice one and I'm driving away from him.

THE ARRANGEMENT

***

THE ARRANGEMENT, Vol. 1
is available now! Buy it today!

***

COMING SOON

To ensure you don't miss H.M. Ward's next book, text **HMWARD** (one word) to **24587** to receive a text reminder on release day.

*****

Want to talk to other fans?
Go to *Facebook* and join the discussion!

MORE FERRO FAMILY BOOKS

JONATHAN FERRO
~STRIPPED~
******

BRYAN FERRO
~THE PROPOSITION~
*****

SEAN FERRO
~THE ARRANGEMENT~
******

PETER FERRO GRANZ
~DAMAGED~
******

NICK FERRO
~THE WEDDING CONTRACT~
*****

MORE ROMANCE BY H.M. WARD

SCANDALOUS

SCANDALOUS 2

SECRETS

THE SECRET LIFE OF TRYSTAN SCOTT

DEMON KISSED

CHRISTMAS KISSES

SECOND CHANCES

And more.

To see a full book list, please visit:
www.sexyawesomebooks.com/#!/BOOKS

CAN'T WAIT FOR H.M. WARD'S NEXT STEAMY BOOK?

★★★★★

Let her know by leaving stars and telling her what
you liked about
MANWHORE
in a review!

COVER REVEAL: